UNDONE

MEGAN LYNCH

CITY OWL
PRESS

UNDONE
Children of the Uprising, Book Three

CITY OWL PRESS
www.cityowlpress.com

Cover Design by Olivia at MiblArt. All stock photos licensed appropriately.

Edited by Amanda Roberts.

For information on subsidiary rights, please contact the publisher at info@cityowlpress.com.

Print Edition ISBN: 978-1-949090-24-6

Digital Edition ISBN: 978-1-949090-23-9

Printed in the United States of America

To My Parents
All of Them—
Julie, Joe, Dianne, and Rich

PRAISE FOR MEGAN LYNCH

"In debut author Lynch's exceptional near-future totalitarian nightmare of obedience and forced sterilization, all major individual decisions are removed. Four central characters in an unnamed city resent their repressive lives...Their lives intertwine in Lynch's scant but complex book, which packs in scathing commentaries on police brutality, crime prevention, population control, classism, and state-sponsored murder."
- Publisher's Weekly

"Instead of broadcasting secret societies and mass uprising as the only hope for an oppressed people, Unregistered focuses on a more personal quest to aid a child convicted of a crime he didn't commit. Unregistered is one of the more innovative and gratifying novels to enter the dystopian genre."
- Readers' Favorite, Caitlin Lyle Farley

"Unregistered is quite engaging, with deep, thought-provoking ideas of government. The book is darkly written, but there are friendships, hope and faith intertwined throughout, which helps offset what is happening."
- InD'tale

"A science fiction story with a lot of heart. I warmed up quickly to all four of the core characters within this grim dystopian world."
- Award Winning Fantasy and Sci-Fi Author, E. J. Wenstrom

CHAPTER ONE

JUDE REEDER WALKED INTO THE CAVERNOUS ROOM AND DREW an even breath. *This is just a simulation,* he reminded himself. *Just do your best.* Even though there were many people already here, the floor plan was so expansive that it almost didn't feel crowded. Almost. He assessed the risks. The only way out was the way he'd come in, through two black sliding doors. There were no windows in the room, which would suggest that the meetings that normally took place here were private, even secretive, though that wasn't quite the case today. Today, the room was packed with young people about Jude's age, which was sixteen. In his training, they'd drilled into Jude to always be five minutes early—any earlier, and he'd be noticed. Any later was, of course, simply too late. Jude found a spot next to the doors and kept looking around, gathering bits of information he might need for later. He moved his eyes from person to person, sneaking glimpses at the faces of the sleek black watches that were wrapped around every wrist.

There were no guards around. They probably didn't expect anyone like Jude to be in the room, only fresh-faced interns eager to please and easy to impress. This was a welcoming ceremony for a whole herd of them in the capital of the United States, after all.

Only a fool—or someone who either had a lot to gain or nothing to lose—would try to sneak in.

When the simulation stage was over and he would finally be sent to the United States, he'd be the only one in a room like this who'd known hardship. However, since camouflage was the key to this entire mission, he'd have to pretend, just for a few months, that he was like the others. That he'd never been compelled to fight for his life. That he had two working hands made of flesh and blood and bone. Not a false one made of wires underneath flesh-colored rubber. In his mother country, where he'd been locked up for being an embarrassment to his government, where citizens voluntarily locked themselves up while consuming government narratives, where he'd miraculously escaped with his mind intact, if not his body, exactly—he would have had to pretend to belong.

None of the other new interns were talking to each other. Most were just looking down at their watches, waiting for the program to start. An empty podium stood on a low stage at the front of the room, and although a few adults were scattered throughout the room talking to each other, Jude hadn't yet guessed who was in charge. He walked along the perimeter, closer to an older man who was talking to a young woman.

"Of course, it's a difficult responsibility, governing the entire world. But every place has resources, and it takes surprisingly little to keep workers alive. We're always working on efficiency. That's why what you're doing is so important." The man's silver hair glimmered in the fluorescents as he turned to Jude, perhaps surprised to find him listening. "And you? Are you an efficiency intern as well?"

Jude fought the urge to hunch over his watch and instead straightened his back and looked at the man's eyes. "Yes."

"Ready for your first day?"

Jude hoped the young woman next to him would respond, but she had already retreated into her wrist. Jude reminded himself of his training: respond casually—and there were concrete ways to be casual. He went with the mirroring technique, crossing his arms and leaning his weight on one leg. "Yes, absolutely."

The man chuckled. "Yes, as you said—absolutely." He uncrossed one of his arms and extended it. "Chuck Pennington."

Jude shook it. "Pleasure to meet you, sir. I'm Dale Downs."

Chuck Pennington looked down at Jude's wrist. "Something the matter with your watch, Dale?"

Jude realized that the man would not let go of his hand. He looked down at his watch to find the face was displaying the "record" icon, threatening to reveal to Chuck Pennington that their conversation was being recorded. Instead of pulling his wrist away, Jude squinted at Chuck's watch. "Yours too?" he asked.

Pennington's eyes and opposite hand instantly shot to his watch to check, while Jude quickly tapped a finger on the screen of his own. "Must have been a reflection," Jude said, but Pennington was already distracted.

"Yes... Good to meet you, Dale." Pennington walked away, eyes on his own watch as he tapped out a little message.

Jude tried to let the interaction go as he took his seat. There was every chance in the world that Pennington had been tapping out a message to his wife, or his child, or a colleague about something that had nothing to do with Jude. They were seconds away from starting the program, but Jude would look suspicious if he simply waited. He opened a game similar to the games being played around him and tapped aimlessly. The game had been a clever design of the engineers back in the UK. It projected false pupils on Jude's eyes to make it seem as if he was focused on his watch, leaving his real eyes free to roam the room. With his head bowed toward the screen, he followed Pennington with his eyes. Pennington tapped his watch once more, gave a nod to someone in the back of the room—Jude turned his head to cough so he could have a look, but didn't see anyone—and took a seat next to the stage.

A young man not much older than Jude took the podium.

"Good morning," he said.

The room rumbled as most of the crowd mumbled their reply.

"Congratulations again on being selected to intern for the worldwide efficiency program. I'm Kyle Belslinger, and I currently have the honor of leading my cohort. By this time next year, one of you will emerge as the leader of yours and will introduce the man responsible for leading all of us to the new recruits." Kyle Belslinger went on for a while about what a great pleasure it was to serve, how much responsibility it was to measure efficiency, how satisfying it was to increase production for those who owned the means, and where the bathrooms were located. Finally, he said, "Please welcome Chuck Pennington, five-star general of the Metrics Worldwide Government and leader of our operation."

The room exploded with applause. Each intern seemed to be trying to make their claps louder than the others. Jude followed suit, cupping his hands to amplify the sound.

"What an honor, what an honor!" Pennington grasped the podium with both hands and thrusted his ribcage over it, dwarfing it as he hovered, and seemed to smile and scowl at once. "Thank you for agreeing to serve in the efficiency program."

Like any of them had a choice, Jude thought, and was silently thankful that he actually did.

"Efficiency is the heart of our society. If productivity is our collective mission in life, using the minimum amount of time and resources is not only a job, but a calling. You are embarking on one of the most important assignments in the entire worldwide system."

Jude fought the urge to roll his eyes and wondered if anyone actually bought this.

"You are helping your fellow human beings by maximizing the quality of their life, which is to say their output. This particular group is so important because you will be the ones working on efficiency in the transportation system. What an exciting opportunity! You will be the ones to study commuter patterns, put yourself in the shoes of a typical Two or Three, and decide which routes to cut and which to expand. You will have responsibility beyond what you'd imagined for yourself, but you will learn to wield it according to Metrics values, for the good of all people."

Heads nodded.

"As I look out at all of you and see your young, fresh faces, I can see—quite understandably—that some of you aren't able to fathom the immense power you've been entrusted with. I'd like to close with a short anecdote to give you a glimpse.

"When I began my career at the Metrics Efficiency Program, Transportation Division, we were still struggling with the issue of pedestrian deaths. Today, pedestrian deaths have become so rare among registered people that it's hard to imagine a time when they were so commonplace. But this was almost thirty years ago now, and it happened so frequently that even Twos would sometimes die in vehicle deaths. When we moved away from individual cars and almost exclusively to trains, we were able to actually save lives with efficiency. The closer to the cities we got—where the higher tiers and their jobs were—the slower the trains could move and the fewer deaths we had. In order for the trains to move slowly enough to stop in emergencies near the cities, the faster we had to speed them up on the outskirts. The transportation department, under our leadership, had an enormous hand in creating the housing plan that accommodates all levels of citizens now. This way, Twos and Threes can live close to their workplaces, and Fours and Fives can get to work quickly without risking their own safety."

A question hung in the air, unasked: And the Unregistered? One of the key policies of the Metrics Worldwide Government was the one-child policy. The second, third, or fourth child in a family was considered Unregistered and received no rights under the law. Prisoners, regardless of their tier, were also automatically classified as Unregistered upon incarceration, which meant that Jude had the unique experience of living as both a Two and an Unregistered. But the government wasn't worldwide at all—though its citizens believed it was. Jude and his friends had discovered that Metrics was a semi-large country that had isolated itself and was now beginning to suffer for resources. The way they found to save resources for all their registered citizens was to murder all of the Unregistered and tell the public that they'd been relocated. Most people in this room probably believed that the Unregistered were still alive and well in a society of their own thousands of miles away from here.

Pennington cleared his throat. "The Unregistered were, up until the relocation, still living in zones where the trains were moving extremely fast in order to transport them to their jobs, if they had one. I was happy when the number of pedestrian deaths declined over the years, but any at all were difficult to accept. And the damage it did to trains was very expensive. I, myself, advocated for their relocation in order to prevent these deaths."

Jude knew it was ridiculous that he was angry after everything that he'd learned, everything that he'd experienced, but he slowed his breathing, remembering the technique Daniel had taught him to control it. He focused on making his exhales longer than his inhales.

"So you see, you have an enormous responsibility in shaping the lives of people all over the world. Be vigilant, but don't be afraid to make tough decisions for the greater good. One could say that it is because of our speeding up and slowing down program that many of you are here today. The time we've saved you in being on the train may have enabled you to study harder, and your parents to earn more to send you to the prestigious schools represented here. Now, do the same—do better, even—for another generation!"

The room thundered with applause, and most of the interns jumped to their feet in an attempt to begin a standing ovation. Jude tried to follow the example of the young leaders and rise, but a hand on his shoulder gently but firmly pressed him back down.

A woman's lips were close to his ear, so close that he could feel her warm breath when she said, "Come with me."

Jude fought the urge to run, fight, or mope, and slowly rose with her hand still on his shoulder. Now he could feel something sharp on his back as the woman led him into the aisle, past the raucous crowd, and back through the sliding black doors. She jabbed the sharp object harder into his back as he stepped through the doors.

Once he was out, he turned, quick and deliberate, grabbed the pointy thing, and looked into the woman's face.

In his good hand, Jude clutched the pencil. Samara glanced down at her own hand, surprised, maybe, that it had been taken so quickly.

"That hurt!" Jude said, and Samara grabbed the pencil back and chuffed him softly.

"Why didn't you check your watch for the icon? We were all waiting for you to do it, but you didn't, and you let Pennington see it! What were you thinking?"

Jude looked down at his watch again and groaned. "It comes back on every few minutes, doesn't it?"

"Yes, it does. You wore one of these for eleven years. How do you not remember this?"

Jude looked at the faces around him. Denver and Stephen were behind Samara, waiting for him to answer. Daniel, still wearing the earpiece, the twin of Jude's, in his own ear, stared at him. More strangers surrounded them, all members of the team that would eventually infiltrate the Metrics government in the attempt to liberate the USA, were staring at him, disappointed by his simple blunder. The United Nations was spending an ungodly amount of money on these training simulations, their eyes seemed to remind him, and he couldn't go screwing it up every time. He needed to prove himself if he wanted to be a part of this team. You didn't need to be perfect to save the world, but you sure as hell had to be competent.

Jude shook his head at the floor. "I'm sorry. Let's go again."

Samara smiled and gave Jude another little jab. "You were doing great before then. But this time, try not to meet Pennington at all. The fewer important people know who you are, the better."

"Got it."

Jude rubbed his back briefly where the pencil point had been stuck, checked his watch, and breathed deeply, his shoulders rising and falling.

The doors opened. He walked inside, where the crowd of young interns were, once again, waiting for their program to begin. He did the same thing as everyone else in the room—checked his watch.

CHAPTER TWO

BRISTOL STEPPED INTO THE NATURAL LIGHT STREAMING FROM A floor-to-ceiling window and looked at a painting while a handful of others—including his agent, Cindy—looked at him. Beside Cindy was a woman who wrote for a magazine, though Bristol didn't exactly know which one because the publication she'd handed him earlier didn't have any words on the cover. A man stood beside her, the curator of the museum. All three watched him intently. He was supposed to be thinking about the painting, which was done by a famous modern artist, but all he could think of was what they were thinking of him. He struck what he hoped looked like a thoughtful pose in front of the frame, curling a hand at the stubble on his chin.

"Any initial thoughts, Mr. Ray?" one of them asked.

Bristol shook his head and kept his eyes on the painting, trying to concentrate.

Cindy clicked her tongue. "He needs to think. What he needs is quiet."

Bristol squinted. His mother used to say, "Nothing good ever happens after midnight," but he found that to be unequivocally untrue. He did his best work after midnight back when he was an

Unregistered citizen, working until the restaurant closed at dark, then going home, grabbing paints and an ice pack to cool the heat-activated monitoring chip in his hand and going to his favorite haunts to paint the new images that had popped into his head during the day. Maybe, for most people, it was sound advice, reminding them to be home and asleep so they could wake up the next day and be productive. But Bristol was anything but normal.

In fact, for Bristol, the exact opposite seemed to be true. "Can I come back tonight?" he asked.

"Well..." the woman started. "You see, we go to print tonight, and our deadline is earlier this evening, and I have to have this finished by then, and—"

"Yes, okay, sorry," he said, and scratched his face. "I think it's great. I like the colors."

The small group of people looked at him blankly. Cindy moved her head from Bristol to the painting. "The...colors?"

"Yes."

"It's...it's just black and white."

Bristol bit his lips together and pointed to a small stroke on the upper right quadrant. "Black and white everywhere except here." He walked up to it and saw what he was actually seeing—the reflection, on a particularly thick stroke of black, where one of the bristles had come loose and was stuck in the paint. It must have caught the light in a strange way, visible only from where he'd been standing before. Now that he saw what it actually was, embarrassment rose up sharply in his throat.

But the others just marveled at the lone bristle hair. "What an eye!" said the curator, whose white hair hung in wisps to the side of his head.

Cindy nudged him. "Bristol also told me how excited he was to see the work of Xiao Lu, because he related to the hardship of creating in an extremist regime."

"Is that right?" asked the woman from the magazine, turning to him.

Bristol nodded. He still wasn't sure how to pronounce the

artist's name, and he didn't want to embarrass himself again by attempting it. "He... We grew up in very different places, but we reacted the same way to being kicked around. I'd like to meet him."

Except that wasn't true. This artist was the real thing while Bristol was just an amateur. What would they have to talk about? But Bristol had to say something and hope that they all let him go home afterward so he could draw sketches no one would see but himself.

Cindy flipped her hair. "We had an extensive conversation about this. I have my notes. Maybe we can let Bristol go and I can tell you what we were talking about earlier?"

Bristol was happy to leave Cindy with the others. From the very beginning, she'd told him, "You just create, and let me do my thing." Except it wasn't quite as simple as that. The art world, he'd learned, was full of people who were willing—no, eager—to spend lots of money on pieces that did not require corresponding effort. Little things he'd make in an afternoon would sell a week later for thousands.

But the money was nice, especially after a lifetime of not having any. He'd bought a flat in Edinburgh, not far from the teahouse where he'd introduced his art to the UK. He lived there happily with his sister, Denver, and her husband, Stephen. Cindy tried, unsuccessfully, to convince him to move to London instead, but Bristol refused. There was still one person who he was working to persuade to move into his flat, but she would not leave Olympic Village, where the American refugees were still being housed.

Bristol cringed as he passed the teahouse on his way home. His picture was still there, on the windowless brick wall. It was only graffiti. He never thought to be critical of his own work, at least not at this level, before Cindy introduced him to real artists. He was self taught, and it showed. He wasn't sure why the pictures he drew seemed to resonate with people who saw them, but he had the feeling that if he was going to continue this lifestyle, he'd better start putting out better work.

But he had no time for better work. The pace of his life overwhelmed him, and everywhere he turned, different groups of people seemed to show up and ask for more. The people who'd come to his shows, dripping in diamonds, would ask him questions about art and politics that they'd obviously spent a lot of time crafting, only to find him unprepared to answer. The Red Sea constantly battered him with talking points to change the public perception of refugees when he did interviews. Even Denver droned on about dishes and dirty laundry, though she and Stephen lived in the flat rent free.

By the time Bristol reached the front door of his building, he was fuming with undirected frustration. He turned the knob and threw open the door, looking forward to plopping down on his leather sofa. He was surprised to find Samara walking across the lobby toward him. He caught his breath.

She smiled at him under the brim of her hat. "Just the person I wanted to see."

"You came here to see me?" In an effort to not sound too excited, he realized he came across as bored. He was quick to correct himself. "It's good to see you." He started to reach his arms out for a hug, but Samara was already looking down at the lobby seating areas. Bristol scratched his chin instead.

"Good to see you too. Anyway, look at this. There's a new public perception poll out. The public's opinion of Clovinger took a slight lean in the other direction."

"Clovinger?"

"Cara Clovinger."

"Cara—?"

"The first minister of Scotland? The woman who is still fighting for us to stay here after four years while even members of her own party are lobbying to have us sent back to the USA and also implement a Metrics-like version of government here?"

"Yeah—okay, I know. So, opinion of her has changed?"

"Just a little bit. Swaying away from her. This doesn't exactly mean their perception of refugees has turned away from us as well, but it doesn't look good. Can you mention something supportive about her when you guys do that magazine interview?"

"Sure."

"That'd be great, because I think phase one of this plan to infiltrate Metrics is going to be fine, but I'm glad they'll only be there a few weeks to start off. We were in simulation training all day and most people did beautifully but I'm worried about Jude..."

As she talked about the minute details of her worries, Bristol sat basking in her presence. Sometimes he liked to imagine that he'd time travelled to this place where they were now, in a part of the world he never knew existed, with this dazzling woman who'd risen to the challenge and had become the Red Sea's liaison with Parliament and the first minister. When they'd met, she was just a girl with interesting thoughts dressed in a drab, dust-covered jacket against the backdrop of her own slum neighborhood. Now, she sat poised at the marble table in this ornate lobby and talked about international politics. Her unruly curls broke away from her bun and formed a cinnamon halo on her head. Some things never changed.

"Maybe you could practice with Jude sometime," she said.

"Practice?"

"Yeah. He was just a kid when we left, so he needs some more practice acting like a Metrics citizen."

"Samara, I was never a Metrics citizen."

She looked at him for a moment like a frightened deer, having been caught in a potentially embarrassing mistake, but when he smiled, she laughed. "I'm so sorry, Bristol. I forgot!"

Bristol laughed too, savoring the release. "If you want him to practice looking at his watch twenty-four/seven, may I suggest my sister as a trainer?"

Samara wiped a burgeoning tear from her eye, still giggling. "I'll talk to her about it. I think she's pretty annoyed with Jude after today, though."

"She'll be home all night. Send him over."

"Okay."

"Maybe you and Jude could both come, and we'll just leave Jude and Denver to practice and we could go out for dinner."

"I'll just send Jude."

"I want to have dinner with you."

"I'll just eat at Olympic Village. It's chili night."

"But there's a new seafood place three blocks from here. I'll pay."

"I like chili." She got up and tugged her hat over her ears. "Do you need me to write up something for you about Clovinger?"

"Yes," he said quickly. "Come over tonight and we can work together on it."

"Bristol—"

"Is seven o'clock good for you?"

"Bristol, we've been through this."

He sighed. "Okay. I'll see you when I see you, Samara."

She gave him a little half-smile and a side hug and was on her way. The way she walked out the door with an understated little swing of her hips as she pulled the door open suggested she knew she was being watched. Bristol watched. When she was gone, he walked to the corner to continue watching as she crossed the street.

When she was really gone, he stepped back, the familiar stench of self-disgust rising inside. The two of them had been a couple briefly, too briefly, back at St. Mary's, the abandoned monastery where the Unregistered hid from the relocation. Back then, they'd had to keep their relationship a secret, and looked forward to the day they could be together, not sneaking around and living in fear, but in the sunlight. But Bristol had come on too strongly too quickly, inexperienced as he was, and Samara had retreated to focus more on making sure they stayed free.

It wasn't until the elevator doors closed in front of Bristol's face that he slapped himself on the forehead. *Stupid.* That interview that she was talking about had ended an hour ago.

CHAPTER THREE

DENVER STEINER TUGGED AT THE FABRIC OF HER HUSBAND'S shirt in her lap. If you folded things correctly, she had read in a homemaking magazine recently, you didn't have to iron. She was willing to try, not because she wanted to be a better homemaker, but because she dearly loved her time and didn't want to waste it. The more steps that could be taken out of something meaningless, like laundry, the better.

The sound of a key entering the front door scraped the air, and Denver's back straightened automatically. Stephen entered, looking at his watch. Denver sagged back into the chair.

"I wish you'd stop wearing that thing."

"Hmm?" He kept his eyes on his wrist.

Denver rose, and Stephen's shirt fell to the floor. She put a hand over his watch, covering it. He snorted and kissed her nose.

"It's good for us," he said.

"It's not."

"Well, it's terrible for us. But we have to practice. There could be an alert that appears for a fraction of a second while we're over there. We have to stay vigilant."

"You know you weren't practicing for the mission."

"That's the reason I married you. Smart as a whip."

"The reason you married me is the same as the reason I married you. Metrics assigned us."

"Even a broken clock is right once a day." He flung his watch on the chair she'd been sitting on and wrapped his arms around her waist. She threaded hers along his back and closed her eyes for a moment, slowing down time. He cleared his throat. She ignored it.

He spoke into her hair. "Jude is coming by tonight to practice."

She tightened her grip on him. "Practice what?"

"Doing things, having conversations—"

She finished his sentence for him, "While looking at a watch."

"And watching for alerts and responding to orders, yes."

"It seems so strange to me that he grew up wearing one and yet can't remember how it's done."

"Muscle memory isn't perfect, I guess."

She sighed, looking toward the basket of yet-to-be-perfectly-folded clothes. "When is he coming?"

"Should be here any minute. I can help you fold."

She resisted the urge to say no—after all, she had a certain way she wanted them done now, and she'd definitely have to redo his sloppy work if he helped. But then the reason she wanted them done that way in the first place—pulled and pressed, like little cloth soldiers standing upright—was so she could have more time with the man she loved before he went to America with the others on the liberation mission.

She picked up the shirt from the floor and nudged the basket toward him with her foot. "Are you just looking for an excuse to touch my underwear?"

He tackled her onto the couch, locked her waist in his arms and turned at the last moment so she would fall on top of him. "We're married. I don't need one."

She laughed and told herself to let them have this moment. It was the least she could do. Still, she longed for reassurance that this wouldn't be the end. "Stephen?"

"Mmm?"

"Promise me something."

"Anything."

"Promise you'll come back."

Stephen cradled her jaw in his hands and pressed his forehead against hers. "I promise."

Immediately, Denver felt disgusted with her words and the overly sentimental, ooey-gooey self he always seemed to bring out of her. "No. You can't promise that."

"But I can! I'll either come back whole and healthy and ready to ravish you—"

"Charming."

"Or I'll find another way."

Denver crossed her arms. "Are you going to haunt me?"

"Oh, like no one's ever been haunted before. Moaning, groaning, rattling chains, the whole thing. I'd just follow you around all day. You better not bring any other guys home, or I'm making some plates fly."

...

Bristol was the one who opened the door for Jude, and even though Denver didn't exactly hear what happened next, she suspected bad news. She knew he was in the mood to sulk after that, because instead of going into his studio, he crept into his bedroom and quietly closed the door. There was a time, long ago, when she could barely keep him in their childhood bedroom that they shared. He'd sneak out almost every night. There was no need for sneaking now.

"Hi, Denver." Jude was unraveling yards of scarf from around his neck. He pulled it a little too tightly, but it stayed put. He coughed. He pulled harder. He coughed again.

"Stop." Denver Ray did not suffer fools. She resisted the urge to march over and tighten it around his neck herself, as opposed to watching him butcher the job. "Let go of the ends. Loosen it at the throat first, then pull it over your head."

Jude hesitated much too long for Denver's liking, but he did follow her instructions and lifted it over his dark curly hair. "Sorry."

"Let's just get to work. Do you have your watch?"

Jude held out his wrist.

"Okay. Stand there. It's really not that hard, Jude. You just have to be more interested in what's on the screen than what's actually going on around you."

"How can I be? Everything inside me is telling me the exact opposite. I feel like it's more important to be aware of my surroundings and—"

"Of course you have to be aware of your surroundings, but you can't stop there. Maybe if we were going on a mission a hundred years ago it would have been important to do that, but now there's more to think about. Being aware of physical danger is just a baseline task now. And you're going to look completely out of place off you're not staring at your watch most of the day."

"It makes my neck hurt."

She set her jaw and forced a breath from her nostrils. "Have you considered that you may not be up for this job?"

"No! I want to help."

"Act like it. Let's start with something easy." She looked down at her watch and opened a game, stacking jewels on top of themselves until they fell over. It had been a favorite before Stephen came along and changed her life. "How was your day?"

"My day was—"

"Open up an easy game first, then talk."

"Oh," Jude fumbled for his wrist. "Uh...Okay. My...day... was...yellow."

"Your day was yellow?"

"Sorry, there are just yellow lasers on here. No, good. My day was good."

Stacking purple on top of green and red on top of purple, Denver asked, "What'd you have for breakfast?"

"Breakfast?"

"Yes. Most important meal of the day. What was it?"

"It—oh, man—it was good."

"I asked what you ate, Jude."

He threw his hands in his lap. "I can't do this. I actually feel myself getting dumber the more I do this."

"That's the idea, little boy. Metrics gave us these, loaded with mindless games, and told us they'd make everything convenient—buying things, gaining intel, connecting with friends. And they did. But they also made us dull. You have to override that. You have to compartmentalize in your brain so your eyes and hands stay down, but your attention stays up." She wanted him to get this so badly. "My husband's life is going to be in your hands. And yours in his. He's really working hard to protect you. Please do the same for him."

Jude sniffed, looked down, and nodded.

They practiced until ten. Jude seemed more energized by the hour, not quite getting the splice between eye, hand, and awareness, but getting much closer. Stephen did a few rounds with him, and Denver watched, conscious of the worry lines deepening in her face but not currently concerned about them.

There was a moment when both of them looked completely natural—both hooked over their watches, carrying on a conversation that was slow but still full of content. A thought struck her. What if their brains betray them and they do, for a critical moment, care more about the game than paying attention to the danger around them? To find out, Denver lunged for Stephen, ready to jab his shoulder.

Stephen immediately put his hand up to catch her first, and put her in a headlock. Denver grinned.

"Finally!" He kissed her head in his arms. "I thought you'd never test me."

Denver wiggled out and turned to Jude. "I'll try to get you next time. Come over tomorrow."

"I don't think I'm ready."

Denver and Stephen spoke at the same time. "Get ready."

CHAPTER FOUR

INSIDE HER ROOM AT OLYMPIC VILLAGE, SAMARA POLISHED HER shoes. She shivered as she held the nude pump in her hands, but her room was so small that she'd opened the little half-window above her twin bed and told herself that she could bear the cold spring air so the entire room wouldn't smell like polish.

She had noticed subtle differences in the way she was treated at Parliament based on the way she looked. Because her cause was of the utmost importance to her—after all, she was saving her own life here, among others—she put the effort in. She polished her shoes, wore lipstick, and painted her nails. She borrowed simple jewelry from the girls at work and used products to smooth her defiant curls into hairstyles similar to how the women wore it here —pale and limp and brushed tightly away from her face.

When her heels were shiny enough—they had been donated, but she felt she wore them well—she put them in the corner and pulled out a giant manila folder of paper. An immigration bill sponsored by a very conservative member of Parliament. Everything she knew about it so far was archaic—not only in content, but also the physical matter. If this were America, the documents would have been hologram projections hovering in the air in front of her nose, not heavy paper that took up most of the space in her bag. Then again, if this were the United States, she wouldn't be able to review legislation at all.

In fact, she was only now just getting used to calling her mother country "the United States." They'd all been told that Metrics was a worldwide government, monitoring every aspect of individual citizens' lives for the greater good of the world. They'd never been told the truth. That the Metrics government had cut off their country and citizens from the rest of the world and managed all the media and connections in order to keep up the illusion.

She'd been naive. After learning about the lies, and even after arriving here in Scotland, she mistakenly thought that all would be well here and she'd finally be free. But there were citizens here— free citizens who had the same access to information she did— who believed their own country would be better off with the isolation and social engineering policies of America. Now, she worked every day to make sure that those citizens didn't get their wish. They didn't understand.

The first day she'd met Cara Clovinger, she was shaking with excitement. She'd been invited back to a semi-private meeting, with the first minister's entourage listening in the background of her expansive office. Clovinger should have been intimidating to Samara. She was dressed that day in subtle Chanel, her suit perfectly tailored to her matronly body. Samara had never smelled perfume like hers on anyone else, but it smelled like money. Behind all of her physical indicators of power, Clovinger had kind eyes that reminded Samara of her own mother. She hoped, one day, to ask Clovinger what had happened to her parents. Were they together? Free? Alive? By now, Samara and Clovinger had built enough of a rapport that she could ask, but she wouldn't just yet. The more she thought about it, the more she wanted time to prepare herself for an honest answer.

Clovinger, in the beginning, had sat down in a floral upholstered chair across from Samara on the love seat. Between them lay an ornate, high-pile rug that was soft even under Samara's shoes.

"Samra?"

Samara cleared her throat. "Actually, Samara."

"Sam-ra?"

"I...I pronounce it Sam-AH-ra."

Clovinger, to her credit, practiced a few more times and eventually got it right. Samara, timid in her new surroundings and suddenly very aware that her own scent screamed white drugstore bar soap, wished for a moment that her parents had named her something more Scottish sounding.

"You have come here to talk about citizenship?"

"Yes," answered Samara, her voice cracking under the pressure of her cause. "We are refugees from a country you call the United States. We understand that we've been granted temporary amnesty, but we'd like to talk about a more permanent solution."

"You have the wrong room, my dear. I completely agree that you and your people should be granted citizenship, if you want it." Clovinger stood, walked to a window, and gestured beyond the decorative iron bars to a nearby building with thick white columns. "You'll have to lobby."

"Lobby, ma'am?"

"Yes, you know, tell the members of Parliament about who you are and why you're here. Ask them to help you stay here. There are a hundred and twenty-nine members of Parliament, and this year, they all care very deeply about the most important issue. Do you know what that is?"

"The most important issue?"

"Yes."

Samara thought about what she'd been hearing at the rallies. What was most important? "Is it defense?"

"No. Have another go."

"Healthcare?"

"No. I'll give you a hint. Not only is it the most important issue, but many regard it as the *only* important issue. No other comes close in terms of priority."

Samara winced. "Immigration?"

"No. Another hint: it was the same issue last year, and the year before. It will be the most important issue next year and ten years from now, it will be the same. Have you guessed yet?"

Samara sat in bewildered silence.

"It is re-election. Find a way to connect your issue, your future, to their re-election, and you will win."

In her little room in Olympic Village, Samara pressed her reading glasses up higher on the bridge of her nose and got to work. It served her well to remember Clovinger's advice before she dug in. She'd learned that potential laws always had two levels—the written and the unwritten. In the unwritten, a wealth of information was available. Who the lawmakers really were. Their background. Their bias. These were the keys to their re-election plans. If you read the unwritten correctly, she thought as she smiled to herself, there was no limit to what you could do.

CHAPTER FIVE

JUDE SMACKED HIS LIPS AS HE SAT HIS TRAY ON THE TABLE. Lunch in Olympic Village wasn't usually stellar, but today the cafeteria was serving his favorite: sausages and boiled potatoes. For most of the fugitive population here, that meant a meal of only potatoes, since many still couldn't stomach the notion of eating dead animals. Jude and his friend Cork were both teenage boys with a lot of growing yet to do, and they'd given up the vegetarian diet they'd grown up with last year.

Jude picked up his fork before he even sat down, but Cork swiped it from his hand. "They're always telling you to practice," he said to Jude. "Do they mean even when you're eating?"

Jude picked up one of the links with his fingers. "Not on sausage day," he said, chewing.

Cork laughed and handed the fork back. "Use a utensil, you animal!"

Jude ate with the fork but noticed he still had Cork's attention. "What?"

"Seriously. Do they eat looking at their watches too?"

"I think so. Probably."

"I feel so dumb that I don't remember, but I really don't."

"We only got them when we were ten, and then I went in Fox County Juvenile Detention Center when I was eleven. I remember them being really cool at first. At school, everyone wanted to synch up their watches to play games with each other. And I remember the girls would spy on the boys with their watches."

"Creeps. How?"

"Don't ask me. I only had a watch for a year. You had one longer than I did. You were almost twelve when you and your brothers went to St. Mary's."

Cork smirked and gazed down at his plate. "Why'd we go to St. Mary's, Jude?"

Jude gulped. Of course. Cork and his little brother, Henry, were Unregistered and not entitled to watches. His oldest brother, Taye, had claimed the citizen status in their family as the firstborn, but he'd taken them to the monastery ahead of the relocation to keep them safe. Taye had been the only one required to give up his watch at the monastery gates; Cork and Henry were never assigned them in the first place. The government had pretended that they'd never been born.

"Sorry."

"No need to be sorry."

Even four years after leaving their home, people here still seemed tied to the old status system. Here, there was absolutely no need to remember who had been Threes, Fours, Fives, and Unregistered. But it had mattered immensely back home, and so much had hinged on that number: culture, education, diet, pretty much every aspect of their lives. Jude was grateful that he, Cork, and Henry had been so young when the relocation happened and had never gotten a real chance to practice condemning others based on their tier. To the adults, it seemed like a mere compulsion.

Cork's eyes kept flitting to Jude's wrist. Jude unfastened it and threw it across the table. "Try it on."

"Bet they'd like that," said Cork, looking over his shoulder for Samara.

True, Samara wouldn't appreciate someone else playing with Jude's watch. It was an expensive piece of training equipment, she'd say. Not a toy. But Jude knew Samara well enough by now not to be afraid of her reaction, especially if he could explain that Cork had never worn one before.

"Just do it. I need someone else to understand how impossible this is."

Cork strapped the little blue band around his wrist and fumbled with the fastener. Jude didn't have the patience to watch him, so he reached across the table and put it on for him.

"Now open World of Sport."

Cork's hand hovered over the face of the watch as if it would puncture his finger if he got too close. "World...of..."

Jude pointed. "Right there."

"Okay. Wow! That was fast."

"Now, you're on the ski jump. You have to drag your finger over there to make the little guy jump and avoid the trees as he goes down the mountain."

It took a few minutes for Cork to get used to it, but as soon as he'd caught on, Jude tried talking to him.

"How are the sausages today?"

"Delicious, as always." Cork popped one into his mouth between swivels of his fingers, no doubt swerving his skier through the forest. "I can't believe they denied us these for so long. If you ask me, that fact alone would convince the Scots that the United States is inhumane."

Jude jutted out his chin as he stared incredulously at his friend. "Are you still playing the game?"

"Winning, I think!" A fanfare of music came from the watch, and Cork punched the air, delighted by the sounds. "Oh, now it's saying I'm onto round two."

"Round two?" Jude didn't know there were rounds in World of Sport.

"Yeah. Oh, oh! Now I'm throwing a stick. Javelin? I'm throwing a javelin."

Jude, annoyed that he couldn't see what a javelin was, took this opportunity to talk more. This was harder than Cork was making it look. "The right-wing members of Parliament would rather never eat meat again than admit that we could be beneficial for their country. How are we beneficial?"

"Oh, lots of ways, I'd think." There were now intermittent cheers coming from the watch. Cork never took his eyes away from the screen. "I've heard people on the news say that we're good for the national fabric. Diversity and all that stuff. Our experience does put us in a unique place. Everybody thinks Samara is so smart, and she is, but mostly I hear what she's saying as common sense. If the people here can't see that, then they really need her around to talk sense into them. And people here are good at some dishes—" He gestured casually to his plate in front of his with his left hand while his right hand elicited more cheers. "But obviously they have no idea how to cook vegetables. We could teach them, open some restaurants, and they'd probably love us for it. But those right-wing guys only care about the economy, and we help there, too. And all the adults work. I'd work too if everybody didn't insist I go to school. I mean, look at Taye. Working down in London with no citizenship. He'll probably have to hire some of those guys that are railing against us someday. Boy, am I looking forward to that day!"

Jude slammed his fists onto the table, and Cork finally looked up.

"How are you doing that?"

"Doing what?"

Cork's confusion only made Jude more embittered. "You're playing that stupid game and talking to me at the same time!"

"Oh...yeah, but it's just a game. Who cares if I win or lose?"

"But you're winning!"

Cork shrugged. "I guess I'm just used to tuning certain things out."

Pouting, Jude grabbed Cork's hand. "Give me that." Jude

opened World of Sports before he'd even strapped on the watch.
"Okay...okay..."

"Just make your eyes and hands stay with the game, but let your
brain stay out here with me," said Cork helpfully.

"Okay...Ask me something."

"How's training going?"

"It's good." His skier crashed into a tree. Jude hung his head.

"Don't get so invested in that. In there, it's just a game.
Who cares?"

"You're right. Okay. Training...is...good..." His skier narrowly
avoided a large boulder and sailed right into a floating gold coin.
How many points was that worth again?

"Hello?" Cork's voice was far away.

Jude sighed. "I hate this. I am so the prototype Metrics citizen;
just give me a watch and I forget about what's important. I don't
know why I'm like this."

"You were bred to be competitive. You were trained to achieve.
Your brain sees a quick and easy chance to win and it can't resist."

Jude considered this. "Yes, but I have inferior genetics.
Breeding didn't work on me."

"How do you know that?"

"I couldn't catch a ball to save my life. I always needed more
time to think about answers to the daily tests. I never had any
friends in school." Admitting these brought a fresh wave of
embarrassment, the old shame new again all these years later.

"You were a late bloomer. If you ask me, Metrics did a great job
with you."

"Thanks, pal."

"It's not your fault, man. I'm just saying it looks like you have a
lot more work to do than, say, I would. Being Unregistered actually
gives you lots of freedom, and a totally different kind of
education."

Jude raked his fingers over his scalp. "You realize you need to
come with me, right?"

Cork made a sound that wasn't quite a laugh. "Me? Go on an international mission? Do you realize I'm failing civics?"

"You're right, though. We have different skills. Right now, it's just me and Stephen going over to stake things out for three weeks. Then we come back for a couple of months, and then the whole team is supposed to go over. Spies from all over the world, all with the mission of liberating America from Metrics. I'm not worried about that second part—those agents know what they're doing. But I'm afraid we'll never get there if I blow it. And the way it's going, I will most definitely blow it. Come with us."

"Jude, it's not like I can just buy a ticket and get on an airship with you."

There was no way he was going to let Cork talk him out of this. Sure, it would make things different, but with him around, Jude would feel bold. Ready. He'd only just gotten the idea and already he couldn't imagine going without him. "I'll talk to them. I'll convince them that you'll be useful. Then you can stare at your watch playing games, and I can stay back and talk to you through an earpiece and let you know how to talk like a Three."

Cork poked a potato. "Well," he said, "I guess it would get me out of school for a few weeks."

CHAPTER SIX

BRISTOL WENT TO CINDY'S APARTMENT WITH A LITANY OF excuses lined up in his head. The pieces she wanted weren't exactly ready, not because he'd been lazy, but because he'd been working on new ones instead. He wished his ideas would just form orderly lines and not come at him all at once, but ever since he'd become a full-time artist, creativity simply took him over in ways he could seldom control. The pieces Cindy had doubtlessly called him over to discuss were commissioned, and although he could always ask for an extension, he never liked to do that when taking money. An agreement was an agreement, and he prided himself on always keeping his end of the bargain. He just wouldn't sleep tonight.

He was prepared to say all these things and more the moment Cindy opened the door, but she called him in and called from the kitchen to ask how many lumps he'd like in his tea.

"None," he answered.

She sighed. "Still?"

"You know I don't like tea."

"Fine. I think I still have some of that horrid instant coffee you insist on..."

Bristol endured a few more mumbled laments about this,

catching familiar phrases like, "How you'd put that stuff in your body." When Cindy finally emerged, holding a mug in either hand, she did not look familiar at all.

Bristol raised his eyebrows. "You look...nice."

"Oh, thank you," she said, eyelashes sweeping downward. "I went to the salon this morning. And I found a tube of lipstick I thought I'd lost in an old coat. And this dress just came back from the cleaners." She stood very close before handing him his coffee.

"I don't have those canvases ready yet," said Bristol, taking a step back.

"That's fine, Bristol. Sit down."

"Okay, but I should probably get going soon to finish those up."

"Sit. I have a present for you."

Bristol blew on his coffee—if it could be called that—and drank prematurely. It burned the middle of his tongue, and in his haste to draw it away from himself, he spilled another scalding drop on his lap. Cindy walked back into the room with a small white box with a blue ribbon tied over it.

"This is from me," she said.

He took it gingerly, wondering how long it had taken to loop the ribbon all those different lengths. "What is it?"

"Just a little something to help further your career," she said.

His stomach dropped. It couldn't be...She wouldn't cross a line so clear. Still, fiancés were technically protected under current law and she could sponsor him until he got his green card. Getting engaged to Scottish colleagues, however, was not a sustainable solution to their particular immigration problem, with almost two hundred American refugees to place. Bristol had always had the feeling that she didn't much care about his countrymen...at least not in the way she cared about him.

He'd just tasted the first hint of vomit in his throat when Cindy asked if he was going to open it. Seeing no other way out, Bristol tugged at one of the blue loops until the whole thing came apart.

He tore at the paper and held his breath as he lifted the top. He looked inside blankly.

"Do you like it?" Cindy asked.

"It's..."

"It's not like those ones where you're from, where they assigned them. It's way nicer than those old models, and it runs faster, too."

Bristol could only stare, stone faced and hard hearted, down at the shimmering silver holowatch that was now his.

"It has all kinds of things loaded on it already, but the thing I want you to pay attention to is a program called Influential Friends."

"Influential Friends?"

"Yes. It's sort of a database for those who have some sort of influence. You go in, create a profile, and you're able to communicate with all sorts of people who are already famous at different levels. I have no idea what level you're at now, but as soon as you create your profile, it will rank you and put you in a pool of people as well-known as you."

"For what purpose?"

"Hold on, I'm getting to that. You can communicate with your rung, and the rungs of famous people beneath you. You'll have to wait for the really famous people to ping you if you want to talk to them. The public can see all your profiles and read them, but they can't ping you directly."

"Ping?"

"Get in contact. No one will bother you, but we need to make you more accessible to the public."

Bristol held the watch at arm's length. "Let me see if I've got this straight. You want me to put this on, make my private information public—"

"Listen to you—private information! Pictures and interests!"

Bristol deeply wanted to tell her that what he considered private wasn't up to her, but he held it in. Reminded himself that she was trying to be nice. Reminded himself to be grateful it wasn't a ring in the box.

"I don't want to be ranked again," he said quietly.

"This isn't like that," she said, placing her hand, greasy from floral-scented lotion, on his. "No matter where you fall on this system, it's good. It only means that people are recognizing you for your hard work. You deserve to be ranked in this program."

He did work hard. And as far as he knew, no one else in the entire camp could do the things that he did. He fulfilled a unique role in this movement to resettle his people. Maybe he did deserve this—and how gratifying it would be to be highly ranked in a fame program after living as an Unregistered his entire life! How inspirational it could be to the others!

Setting up the watch for himself took much longer than he would have guessed. He was at Cindy's long after his coffee went cold, and when the sun set, he was still there uploading photos of himself and his art.

"That was a fun night," said Cindy as a photo of the two of them popped up on the screen. She changed her voice, made it deeper and more commanding. "Watch—show us, eight hundred percent."

A hologram of the two of them shot out from Bristol's wrist, and an image of the two of them appeared in her living room. A slightly opaque Bristol, in his gray tweed suit jacket and plum shirt, Cindy hanging from his shoulder, though she'd barely known him at the time. The snapshot was from an art exhibition nearly four years ago. Bristol smiled as he remembered what had happened later that same night—Jude had come and told him that Samara was missing, and the two of them looked all night for her. When they'd eventually found her, she'd told them that she'd been striking up a friendship with the first minister. The girl had always been full of surprises.

"You clean up well, I must say." Cindy lingered near the hologram, almost touching it. "We look happy."

Bristol chuckled. "I had to get an aid worker at Olympic Village to show me how to tie that tie. I'd never done it before."

"Coulda fooled me."

Why did she always insist on saying things in that tone?

"Tell me what I owe you for this," he said. He tapped the face of the watch to cut off the hologram and privately congratulated himself on being a fast learner.

"It's a gift."

"Really, what?"

"A gift! Ever heard of them? They're free of charge."

Bristol hoped she'd put it on her expense report.

On the walk home, the watch felt substantial on his wrist. Heavy. Expensive.

The program had ranked him in the second-lowest rung of fame. Definitely more famous than the average person, but there were very ordinary looking people in his rung. Real estate agents and business owners and the like. He felt he should be more famous than them—all for the cause, of course. The real reason behind any of this was to gain citizenship for their faction. As long as he was well-known enough to keep his countrymen here long enough for the rest of the world's armies to liberate the United States, that was all he cared about. Then maybe he could see his mom again. If that wasn't a good enough reason to wish for fame, he didn't know what was.

The last time he'd seen his mother, Bristol had been more focused on what he did best back then: sneaking away from her. He'd been out all night, checking Samara's window for signs of life inside, dabbling with a stencil on the familiar brick wall below. He needed to be back before the sun rose for two reasons. One, to not get caught as an unlicensed artist, and two, to make sure his mom saw him before she left for work. He didn't think she was suspicious—she was too tired to be—but he knew she'd be heartbroken and sick with worry if she ever did suspect he was doing anything other than sleeping in his own bed every night. He slipped in through the bars of his window, put on his pajamas, and went to the bathroom to scrub the paint from his fingernails.

That morning, that last morning, she'd been awake at the table when he'd come out of his room. He hid his hands inside the sleeves of his sweatshirt.

"Morning, my love," she'd said and kissed his forehead.

Bristol remembered very little else. Denver had moved into marriage housing with Stephen by then, so it had just been the two of them. Did they have coffee together that last day? Did they talk about anything? Had Bristol's last conversation with her been lies about how well he'd slept? They both had gone to work. Bristol had never come back.

Over the years, he'd tried hard not to imagine the day. Even now, the more he tried to block it, the more his imagination bullied its way to the forefront of his mind. He saw her at her desk, listening to coworkers whisper about the relocation. He imagined her at her window at work, watching police take the Unregistered janitorial staff away from the office park in armored vans. He saw her, panicked, rushing home to find an empty apartment, diving into his rumbled sheets, clutching his discarded sweatshirt to her heart, crying and moaning and screaming for it to be yesterday, for him to come back. He could see it vividly, because it's what she'd done when the policeman had come to their house years earlier and told her that her husband had been hit by a train.

Bristol rubbed his eyes. He would become famous and bring her to Edinburgh. She could live with her two children again in his flat. They'd all sit at the dinner table and laugh about these pale people and their funny accents and colorful money and hefty food.

Just stay the course, he told himself. Just keep going.

CHAPTER SEVEN

IT WAS A NICE DAY FOR A WALK THROUGH THE CEMETERY. Denver had taken plenty of walks through gloomy drizzle and biting wind, which were both satisfying in their own ways, reflecting her own heartbrokenness at having to visit her son's gravesite in the first place. But when the sun was shining, she felt more inclined to recall the happy memories of carrying him.

Some do-gooders in the city, of which there seemed to be many despite the loudness of the opposite faction (the do-badders?), had offered to bury him here with the other babies, though he wasn't fully developed. She hadn't even been halfway through her pregnancy when she miscarried him, but she did get to hold him in her hands, she did get to name him. His name on his little gravestone gave her a morbid kind of pride every time she came here to read it: Zion Steiner. She smiled as she approached it. Though the sun was shining, the grass was still wet from the night before. She sat anyway and placed her hand lovingly on the earth.

"Hello," she whispered.

It seemed to her to be a timeless place, a still place. Life went on outside these stone walls, but the bodies inside rested, hopefully, in peace. It was impossible not to catch some of that peace, Denver thought. She suggested to Stephen that he come and spend some time here whenever he felt stressed, but he always seemed to be too busy. Sometimes it was difficult to be still, like her little boy in the ground. Stephen didn't like to think about losing him.

After Zion's death, Denver went to the doctor for a birth control implant. Neither Stephen nor Denver had brought up the subject of children again until Stephen asked if he could go on the mission with the first round of spies.

"If you go," Denver had said, "could it be the only time?"

"Yes," he said. "They assured me it would be just this one time."

"And then—do you think you'd have built up enough goodwill for us to stay here in the city? Even if it's just us?"

"I think so."

"And then—" She wondered if she should finish.

"Yes," he'd answered.

"Yes, what?"

"Yes, then we could try for another child."

She'd never told anyone else about this conversation—especially not Bristol, whom she knew already saw her as too self-interested—but she needed all of this to be true, everything from Stephen coming back after one trip and never returning to staying here in Edinburgh forever. Though none of it seemed likely, her experience over the last few years had taught her to see hope not as a sappy daydream, but as a tool for survival.

She cleared her throat again and pressed on the ground. "Your daddy is going on a business trip next week. He promised he'd come see you before he leaves. But he'll be back, and then we'll all be here in the city. Someday we'll buy an apartment ourselves, right next door to here. And then mama can come see you every day. And I'll bring your brother or sister. Only a few more years to go now."

A buzzing sound cut through the stillness and Denver bristled. Of course they'd choose the first nice day of spring to do maintenance work here, mourners be damned. The buzzing got closer and closer until she could see the gardener out of the corner of her eye, watching her.

She smiled back at her son's little piece of earth. "I'll have to come back here tomorrow," she told him. "Your stone is going to get all messy with the grass. But you'll probably like the way it smells."

She looked at the date under his name. There was just one: the day she'd miscarried. She did a quick calculation based on when he would have been born and figured he would have been three and a half by now.

The gardener kept staring at her. She appreciated that he was waiting for her to leave before he came into the infant yard with his weed-eater, but she wished he'd turn it off while he waited. She was never ready to leave Zion.

"Bye," she said, allowing the guilt, familiar and weighty, to wash over her as she walked away.

She couldn't go home yet. Stephen would be back soon, but she needed some time to gather herself before she saw him. The weeks before they both went off to London for training were always notorious for arguments. This week, they'd both been treading lightly around each other to avoid them. She went to Olympic Village, hoping to find Samara.

Samara's door was unlocked. She sat hunched over a stack of papers the height of Denver's forearm. Denver looked at the stack, and then at Samara's hollow face.

"Want a break?" Denver asked.

"I'm just trying to get a rhythm going. I should be able to understand this."

"Isn't that stuff written for the sole purpose of people like us not being able to understand it?"

"That's exactly why it's important that we do."

"You need a drink."

Samara stood and rolled her shoulders until they popped. "I think you need a drink. But I'm happy to enable you."

Denver knew Samara didn't like to be seen out at pubs, so she'd bought a little bottle of Rosé on the way over. She pulled it from her bag, along with two paper cups.

"How are you with all this?"

"Oh, I'm happy to play homemaker while my brother expresses himself and my husband goes to war." Denver was aware that she always seemed hostile around Samara, though she was her only female friend here. She hadn't yet been able to shake the habit.

Samara cut her sip short. "Okay, none of that is true."

"No? I'm home all day, cleaning—"

"—You work sixteen-hour days on the weeks you spend training the infiltration recruits."

"And Bristol paints and talks about his paintings with every weird art person in the city—"

"—He's in the public eye to educate them about our situation."

"And Stephen is leaving next week for a country that tried to kill us all."

"Just to plant a couple of surveillance devices." Samara reached for the bottle to pour more wine into Denver's cup. "This isn't the end."

"You know how dangerous it is." Denver stared at her own reflection in the pink liquid. "The commander said to prepare myself for the fact that he may not come back."

Samara opened her mouth to say something but took a drink instead. She was a terrible actor, but at least she wouldn't lie to her.

"So, tell me there's good news in that," Denver said, pointing to the papers on Samara's desk.

"Well," said Samara, "there's news, anyway. There's a bill being introduced now to stop immigration to Scotland except in cases where 'the skills of the migrant would be beneficial to the country's economy.'"

"What's the problem with that? Most of us are educated, at least mostly so. I'd love to finish my training and work as an architect here."

"But they'd have to make an initial investment in you to finish your training, and they see that as a waste of money."

Denver frowned. "But I see these kids on the street all the time, watching football and wasting their time in bars. The government is making investments in their education, aren't they?"

"They were born here. They can waste their opportunity if they want to."

Denver looked out Samara's little window to stare at the rooftop. "It's just like home, isn't it? People putting themselves up on a peak just to look down at the valley."

Samara closed her eyes. "I've been trying to see it from their right point of view. They pay their taxes to educate their own children, ensure that they themselves can drive on the roads, and protect themselves with their own police force. They didn't account for taking care of anyone other than themselves."

"It won't be long before their own 'relocation' if that's their viewpoint. That money is more valuable than people."

"I don't think most of them truly understand that sending us back would be killing us. I've talked to these people, and I don't think they really want to kill us."

"They just don't care what happens to us."

"Well, yes. I think they'd rather see us go to another host country first, but mostly they just want us out."

Denver downed the rest of her wine. "I guess it's best that we go through with it then. All of it. Stephen and Jude planting the devices, the armies toppling the USA's regime. Though I do miss it."

"I miss home, too. I just want it to be safer. A little more like here."

"There are bad people everywhere. I don't want it to be perfect, I just want to live somewhere where I can live my life."

Samara shuffled the papers slowly. "Did you visit Zion today?"

Defensiveness abruptly rose in Denver's chest. "Why do you ask?"

"That's always what you want after the cemetery. Just a place to live your life."

Denver felt blood rushing to her cheeks. "It teaches me what's important."

"I know. At least I think I know. It's good to be reminded of that too. I don't much care whether we ever go home or not. I want everyone in America to be safe, and I know they're not right now. But I'm keeping my expectations low. As long as we have a place to live, safely, I'll be satisfied."

Denver thought of the cemetery, of her little boy's body in the ground. Of just the two of them in the country when Stephen left, even if only for a few weeks. She was afraid Stephen would soon be in the ground in another country, the two of them separated forever. She was afraid her mother was already and she'd never find out for sure. She was afraid she'd never be satisfied.

CHAPTER EIGHT

SAMARA HUFFED AS SHE TOOK THE STEPS TO THE CAPITOL building two at a time. She could not be late for her meeting with Clovinger.

Initially, the intelligence agencies of the UK had assured Samara and the others that it was a very simple plan: take just two refugees—they'd chosen Jude and Stephen—with one escort from the agency. They'd plant a few devices so that the agencies could listen in and gather intel for a few weeks. Then, when they were certain it was safe to do so, they'd go over as a team, in larger and larger numbers until there were enough of them there to bring down Metrics and slowly reintroduce democracy to the United States.

Samara, at first, had thought the logistics for phase II were a little too vague, but she reconsidered; after all, as long as phase I was executed perfectly, there was time to think it all through.

But plans were unraveling quickly.

Jude had come to Samara and asked if his friend could come. She bristled and told him this wasn't a sleepover.

"It's a dangerous mission," she said, keeping her voice firm even though she knew from looking at Jude's face that his argument was far from over.

"He can use his watch better than I can. But I'll be more adept at talking like a Two. If I can do the talking, I can get us access to our targets and he can gather intel once we're there."

"You're not there to gather intel. You're literally just there to gain access and plant devices. If you're concerned about not being able to talk and work at the same time, I can practice with you again."

"It's no use. I'm seriously dysfunctional when it comes to that skill, and it's necessary for communicating there. But I'm also the only Two, and I'll need someone with me who can—"

"Stephen will be with you. And you'll have an escort from the agency."

"Someone who is the same age so he can come with me to the Young Transportation Officials meeting. Cork can do it."

"Cork doesn't have the training. And even if he did, none of the infrastructure is in place for him. They've been working on constructing three fake metrics identities for months, and there's not time to make another one."

Jude crossed his arms and furrowed his brow. "I'm at least going to bring it up to the agency. He could be a great resource. I could be dead without him."

"You could be dead anyway. But if it's so important to you, bring it up with them."

She was sure their answer would be no, and it wasn't long before her suspicions were confirmed. The person who brought it up to her was none other than her old friend the first minister.

Although Samara had a bi-monthly meeting with Cara Clovinger, she was careful not to take her time with the most powerful woman in the country for granted. She never came to the twenty-minute meeting without an agenda and notes that she could quickly glance at no matter which way the conversation veered. When Samara arrived at the State building, she was surprised to find that it was Clovinger who had the agenda.

"Miss Shepherd."

Samara clutched the handle of her second-hand briefcase, taken aback by the formality and the tone. She instinctively took on the posture of her teenage years: shoulders hung forward, hands together at her waist, eyes wide. "Ma'am?"

"I hope I have been misinformed about this. Did you tell your young friend Jude Reeder to pester my intelligence agencies to bring one of his mates on the mission?"

Samara swayed on her feet. "I..."

"Because if you did, I consider it to be very poor judgement on your part. In fact, I'd consider asking you to recommend another refugee to be my liaison to your community."

Struck dumb by a crushing shame, Samara grasped for words. "I'm so sorry..."

Clovinger, usually a reserved woman, slammed her fist into her gleaming desk. "You and this child must think this is a game! We are attempting to liberate your country with our own people. Lives are at stake, Miss Shepherd! How dare you encourage teenage idiocrasy like this?"

Samara held her breath, finally collected enough to be angry and sound enough not to show it. "I did try to convince him that it was a bad idea, ma'am, but he insisted. There was nothing I could have done to stop him from at least asking the team."

"My intelligence officers are not the boy's mother."

"Neither am I, ma'am."

As soon as it escaped her mouth, Samara regretted it. Clovinger turned slowly, in a way that eerily reminded her of someone else: Warden Paul, head of Fox County Juvenile Detention Center, where Samara met Jude and began her years-long habit of defending his trouble making. The regret was then replaced with something else, something ferocious. She still thought Jude's idea to bring Cork along was a terrible one, but there had been too many adults standing in Jude's way. As important as Clovinger was, Samara wouldn't allow her to call Jude names. She stood straight.

"I think it's time for you to go, Miss Shepherd."

"Yes, ma'am."

Clovinger was the first to turn away, perhaps desiring to make a dramatic exit while remaining in the same room. She walked behind her desk as Samara walked back through the door and into the marble hallway.

She didn't catch her breath again until she was halfway down the long outdoor walkway. She wanted to immediately confront Jude, talk to Stephen, commiserate with Denver, ask Bristol if this was all for the best. She remembered life with her watch. When she had one, she was instantly connected to all of the people in her life and this feeling was largely absent. Samara had never allowed feelings to last long because they didn't have to last. She could just message someone, call someone, or open a program, and the feelings would morph into something else. Anger would turn to vindication, sadness to comfort, boredom to stimulation. She could have a watch here if she wanted it, but she'd gotten used to this new way of life, and sitting with these feelings, prodding them and looking at them from different angles, did something to her brain she recognized as good.

Usually. But today was different. When she was confident that she was out of sight of Clovinger's window, she bolted. And she didn't stop running until she reached Bristol's apartment.

CHAPTER NINE

BRISTOL DIDN'T EVEN BREAK HIS STARE ON THE CANVAS WHEN HE heard the door open, thinking—or maybe not thinking at all—that it was just his sister or brother-in-law. When he heard Samara's voice calling him, however, he jumped to his feet so quickly that the palate crashed to the floor.

She was at his bedroom door before he knew it. Face red, hair disheveled, and shirt stained dark at the armpits, everything about her appearance waved a red flag in Bristol's mind.

"What's wrong?"

"Clovinger...Jude..." She threw her briefcase on his bed, then herself. "Just give me a minute."

During the excruciating moments while she caught her breath, Bristol sat back down on the chair and wrung his hands, trying to guess what could rattle her like this. Finally, she put her feet on the ground and told him what happened.

"I just feel tired," she said when she was done. "I feel tired of trying so damn hard. I'm tired of caring. I want to go back to playing games and worrying about grades. I want to eat a dinner that my mom made. I want to talk to my dad about nothing again.

I want to go back to *wishing* I had a big life instead of actually *having* one."

Bristol nodded. "I feel the same way."

"We didn't have freedom, but we had comfort." She seemed to catch herself and turned away. "At least I did. I didn't appreciate it."

"No, I did too. But I can't think too much about what I've lost. It gets me in a depression and it's hard to get out. It helps me to live with a little bit of denial."

"It's exhausting to fight for your life."

"That's not what they think we're doing. That's why it's so easy to deny us. It's like The Fat Man and The Loop.

"The Fat Man?"

"And The Loop. Just—what'd Denver call it? A morality exercise. Say a trolley is hurling towards a group of people, but you're on a bridge where the trolley will pass and realize that if you push something heavy down onto the track, it will stop it from killing all those people. But the only heavy thing next to you is a fat man. Most people say they wouldn't push him down—they would never be able to do something like that. But there's a variant called The Loop. If you ask someone whether they'd pull a lever to divert the trolley, even if that same fat man is on the opposite track and will be killed, most people say they'd still pull the lever to save the group of people. Pulling a lever doesn't seem like killing."

"Clovinger's pulling the lever."

"No, Clovinger will come around. She's smart, and she won't stay mad forever. She realizes that to cut you off is to kill us. We just have to convince the population here that sending us back is a death sentence that they themselves are signing."

Samara fell back on the bed, curled her legs into her body, and turned to her side, eyes closed. Bristol's heart thumped at the sight of her.

"I need a break."

"Take one."

Samara's chest rose and fell, but she kept her eyes closed. "What are you working on?"

Bristol's cheeks prickled. "Nothing."

"What?"

"It's not ready."

"Since when has that stopped you from showing me?"

He hated when she said things like that. It was only four years ago that he asked her to marry him—and she'd refused. Neither of them had dated anyone else since then. There was no way she didn't realize the weight her words carried. But then she opened her eyes and looked up at him, her curls still spread out on his quilt. He sighed and turned the canvas to her.

She gasped and sat up.

He didn't really consider himself a realist. Especially in the past few years, his art had become more and more conceptual. But he couldn't get this image out of his mind, and for a week now, he had striven to paint it with the most detail he could muster.

"What's it called?" she asked.

"I'm thinking of calling it 'Portrait of a Grieving Mother.'"

On the canvas, his mother—the image of his mother—was crouched in the kitchen of his old apartment, fingers dug into her scalp, while her face was caught in a scream. But instead of tightening her face, he'd loosened it, trying to make it look like the scream was coming from within, from some deep and secret place, that she'd just received news that made it impossible not to scream. Working on it had been wrenching. He was sure, with every stroke, that he was painting what was once a true moment. This had been the worst week of his life since arriving in Edinburgh.

Samara looked without speaking for a long time, until Bristol began to see it through her eyes. His mother, screaming low and slow, longing for her children. His eyes became wet. Finally, Samara reached out and cupped his cheek with her hand. He turned his face toward hers, but he didn't want to look at her. She came in from below and kissed him, the same as he'd remembered it for all those years ago: soft.

He kept his hands at his sides, even as she ran hers across his hips. "Samara," he said.

"Mmhmm?"

"This isn't right."

"It feels right to me." She nuzzled at his neck.

He didn't want her like this—in a moment of weakness, as a distraction from their lives—but he didn't have the strength to resist her. He pulled her body tighter into his with his right hand as he switched off the lights with his left.

CHAPTER TEN

JUDE COULD SEE THAT CORK WAS UNCOMFORTABLE AS SOON AS HE told him the new plan. But Jude had done too much to quit now: in ten days, he'd stolen a watch, programed it with a fake identity, hacked the Metrics database to register Cork's new identity as a Two, and made sure that the launch team had read a memo—supposedly from the general—to allow Cork on Jude's airship. The days when he deferred to others were long over. He'd noticed, even at sixteen, that he was often the sharpest person in the room. Talking while on a watch notwithstanding, of course.

"This is going to work," said Jude. "No one believes me, but I need you there."

"You've hacked into Metrics—why the heck would you still need me? All I can do is talk and play dumb games."

"That's the only way to communicate with them! I'm going to be dead in five minutes without someone who can do it. All I have to do is pretend to be shy while you distract them, and then I'll plant all the devices while you game and gab. They'll thank us when we all come home alive."

"And if we don't?"

"That's not going to happen." Jude handed him his new watch.

"We leave tomorrow. And there's no way I can do this without you."

"They think Stephen is going to help you."

"I've told them, many times, that Stephen is going to be with me everywhere except the Young Transportation Officials meeting. And that's what I'm worried about. I've already registered you in their database."

"Have you at least told Stephen about this?"

"He's going over on a separate airship, so we'll meet him at the hotel."

"So, no."

"Not yet. But once he sees you at the hotel, he'll be on board."

Cork sunk his head back, exposing his bourgeoning Adam's apple to the ceiling of Jude's room. "He should know, at the very least."

"The less he knows, the better. He could get in trouble if word gets out before we go over."

"What, and you won't?"

"Oh, I'd be in a lot of trouble if I didn't know how to cover my tracks. I've got this. I've double and triple and quadruple checked." Jude searched his friend's face, trying hard to find more confidence. The truth was that Cork had become more than a friend, more, even, than a brother. Jude wasn't sure what he wanted of him exactly, he just knew that the two of them should be together. He sucked on his lower lip. "I...I really can't do this without you."

Cork's face slowly transformed into a half-grin. "What time tomorrow?"

"Meet me downstairs at dawn."

Stephen came to visit shortly after Cork left. Jude knew it was him from the soft knock on his dorm door.

"Come in."

"It's me," Stephen said, stepping in. He held a brown bag stamped with the name of Jude's favorite tea shop. "Brought some chocolate pastries."

Jude cleared a spot on his desk and offered Stephen the chair. Stephen pulled out a flaky treat and put it on a napkin in front of Jude. "I wanted to check in with you, make sure you were okay."

"I'm okay," Jude said, not touching the pastry. The scent of it was alluring, but he suddenly felt both afraid and very guilty now that Stephen was here, in the flesh.

"I know that it's scary," said Stephen. "And I know how you've struggled. But you can do this. And this is the start of something big. Jude, I don't think I'm being hyperbolic when I say that we're about to change history."

"I know."

Stephen grinned and bit into his pastry. "Well, it's good to be around someone who is also changing history tomorrow." He nodded at Jude's treat. "D'ya think I poisoned that? You're gonna be a great spy someday."

Jude snickered, thinking, *You have no idea*, but picked up his pastry and took a big bite, trying to get rid of it—and Stephen—as soon as possible. "What does Denver think of you coming to check on me?"

"Oh, this is the first she's let me out of her sight all day. We walked here together. She's downstairs having one of these with Samara. Or at least that was the idea. She hasn't eaten anything today."

"Better get back down to her then." He stuffed the rest into his mouth, then spoke thickly. "We should get to bed."

"Okay, Jude. You're probably right." Stephen stood up, placing his half-eaten pastry back into the bag. "But since my airship is leaving first and I won't see you again until we're on the other side, I wanted to tell you something."

Jude wanted his room back. "What?"

"You're much more capable than you think you are. And you're braver than you believe too. I'm proud of you."

Jude's face burned and the chocolate threatened to come back up his throat. "Thank you."

"No problem." He moved in for an awkward hug. Jude stuck his arms out and gave him a little pat on the shoulder while Stephen locked him in. "Well…see you over there."

Jude's stomach lurched as Stephen turned to go. "Stephen?"

He turned around. "Yep?"

Jude sucked in some air. "Good…luck."

"Good luck to you, Jude."

The door closed behind him gently. After a bewildered moment, the floor swayed, and Jude grabbed the little trashcan under his desk to vomit into it.

Cork met him at dawn, as planned. An unmarked car picked up both boys, and though the driver of the vehicle was surprised to see two boys there, Jude asked him to check his messages, and sure enough, the driver had the fake memo from the general. All checked out. None of them said much on the three-hour ride far into the countryside, until the car stopped at a nondescript air field and dropped them off. Jude held his breath as a soldier opened his door. No one seemed surprised when Cork slid out of the seat too.

One of the spies, a member of the launch team, stepped off the medium-sized black airship, shimmering like a mirror, and approached them. "Boys ready?"

Jude nodded, not daring to look at Cork. Without another word, he turned and walked back toward the airship. They followed.

The inside looked quite different from the airship they'd come over on. That one must have been a cargo ship, Jude thought. The inside of that first ship was expansive, and they all sat on the floor. There hadn't been any windows. This one was the same shape—round—but it had a smaller circumference. There was a semi-circle of gray seats, and they could see that when the hatch closed, there would be a large window to look out from the semi-circle. Jude and Cork sat in the middle.

The launch team spy nodded at them. "This ship's programmed to land about forty minutes outside of the city. The directions to the hotel will appear on your watches. All the best, boys." He closed the hatch.

Jude and Cork didn't look at each other until the ship began to hover above the ground. Jude had never seen Cork look so white before. Neither of them was particularly experienced at this sensation, but they knew what was coming next. The airship suddenly flew straight up into the sky smooth enough, but it was still able to jolt their systems.

"I think I'm gonna throw up," said Cork.

"You won't. The worst is over. We won't feel anything else until the descent."

"How long do you think until we get there?"

"It's a four-hour flight," said Jude, but before he finished his sentence, they were already descending. It was the same as he remembered it—slow, but distinct—his ears even popped again.

Cork looked terrified. "Maybe they forgot to tell us something?"

No, thought Jude, no no no no.

The same spy as they'd just approached the window and opened the hatch. "We're aborting the mission. I regret to inform you that we've been compromised."

Jude gulped. "Compromised?"

"We just received confirmation that Stephen's airship has been shot down."

CHAPTER ELEVEN

WHEN DENVER SAW THE TWO MEN IN TRENCH COATS APPROACH her building from the window, she thought, *Oh, there they are.* She didn't expect them to come so quickly, but there was a piece of her that did expect them.

They told her that her husband had died as soon as his airship had crossed over into Metrics airspace, and she nodded. Since Bristol was out, they asked her if there was anyone they could call to be with her.

"No thank you," she said. "I'm sure someone will be here soon. I'd like to be alone now."

They nodded respectfully, and showed themselves out. Breath seemed to freeze in Denver's lungs. Feeling outside of her body, she was aware of herself crossing the room and crouching down on the floor.

Haunt me, she pleaded in her mind. *Haunt me.*

But no one answered. Her child was in the ground and her husband was burned and broken into pieces, probably floating in the Atlantic Ocean. Earth and water. She was alone in the air.

Samara came sometime after the men had left, but how long after, Denver could not say. An hour? Three? Five? She lay on the thin woven rug with her arms and legs spayed outward and listened to the knock. Just from the sound of the fist on the door, she knew it was Samara, so she did not get up. She wanted to see her, and she knew that Samara would come in anyway, even if she didn't answer. She was right.

Samara kneeled down and lifted Denver's head into her lap.

Denver's thoughts ran into each other in her head, so much so that she had the urge to say them out loud, just to pick them out of the mix and clear her mind. So after a prolonged silence, Denver said, "It's the guilt that stings the most."

"You have nothing to feel guilty about," said Samara in a low voice.

"I do. It was a mistake to let him go, but I made a bigger mistake before that."

"You haven't made any mistakes, Denver."

"Will you stop that? Yes, I have. I let myself be fooled by him in the very beginning of our marriage, when I was convinced that Metrics was punishing me for my mom's rule breaking. I thought he was a loser, working late and then spending all evening playing games on his watch instead of showing interest in us. He was actually coordinating with the Red Sea. Those first months were wasted. I wasted them. I didn't know—" She wanted to say she didn't know how precious the time had been, but her throat was blocked.

Samara gently traced Denver's eyebrow with her middle finger. "That's just it. You didn't know."

The real twist of the knife was planning the funeral. The funeral director was a sad-looking man whose face appeared permanently stretched downward, basset hound style, from the years of mirroring the faces of bereaved families. Though he nailed the facial expression, he came off as anything but sincere whenever he opened his mouth.

"Mrs. Steiner," he said, cupping her hand in both of his, "I'm so sorry to hear about the loss of your husband. I'm told it was an automobile accident? I have it there are no remains to be buried?"

"Yes, the car was totaled and just went up in flames." She was glad the tears weren't far behind as she repeated the lie the agency had taught her. They seemed to deter him.

"We'll have a lovely memorial service then," he said. "Pardon what may seem like callousness, but we do have to talk expenses. How much are you prepared to spend?"

When Denver told him, he gave a little flummoxed chuckle. "Mrs. Steiner," he said, "with that amount, we could have a service, yes, but please consider that the little extras really make the legacy of the dead more…meaningful. For example, for an extra thousand, you could have a little reel of holovideos from his entire life playing as your guests enter."

"All his baby holovideos are back in America. We're refugees."

"Recent ones, then. And then an additional twelve-hundred would ensure that there are valet drivers at the door—"

"Not many of us have a need for valet parking."

"All right, all right. At least consider hosting a memorial luncheon, where his friends can be together and talk of the finest memories they hold of dear Steve Steiner."

"His name is Stephen." Denver gritted her teeth. As much as she wanted to tell this guy to buzz off and let her grieve without trying to wring more of Bristol's money out of her, appearing to be cheap also felt disrespectful to Stephen's memory. What would he have done if it had been her? Oh, why couldn't it have been her? "I'm sorry. Can I give you a call a little later today? I thought I was ready, but I'm not."

He did a little half-bow as the corners of his mouth sagged downward. "Of course. I'll be available this afternoon."

On the walk home, Denver's heart hurt. Literally hurt. She stopped and sat on a bench at one point, trying to remember whether or not she'd learned the symptoms of a heart attack. Was it breathlessness? She was certainly breathless. A feeling of dread? Vision jolting? If this was a heart attack, she welcomed it, but she had the suspicion that it was nothing but her world falling into pieces without Stephen.

Stephen. The only one who'd ever made her feel whole. Chosen. Cherished. The reason she'd survived this long. She wanted nothing more than to turn back time. She wanted to be with him again in the woods, running from Metrics. He had been so sick, and she'd never before taken care of someone so fervently, wanting them to get better with everything inside her. She wanted to go back to when they'd first arrived at St. Mary's, the Unregistered hideaway in the hills not far from the city, where they'd sneak away to make love to each other, thrilled that they no longer had to log their activity for Metrics' records. She wanted to go back to Olympic Village, with their baby growing inside her and the freedom to do what they'd never fully been able to do—get to know each other. She wanted to go back to the train rides to London for training and the lazy weekend mornings in bed and even the last walk home together, when both of their palms were so sweaty that they'd given up on holding hands and threaded their arms around each other to walk instead.

An older man waiting for the bus asked if she was okay, and instead of answering him, she slumped downward and hoped he'd go away.

"Hmph! How d'ya like that?" he said loudly. "Seems about right —an immigrant who won't show basic respect!"

She wanted nothing more than to rise up and slap his face. But Stephen didn't die so that his cause would be negated. It was up to her, both in big ways and in small, to make sure his death wasn't in vain.

She straightened up and smiled. "I'm sorry, sir. I didn't realize you were speaking to me. I have a bit of a cold today, but I'm just fine. Thank you for asking."

The man hmphed again and hurried away. Denver looked after him and silently thanked him. He didn't know it, but he had just charged her with a new mission: carrying on her husband's legacy.

CHAPTER TWELVE

SAMARA HAD ASKED IF SHE COULD SPEAK AT THE MEMORIAL service. Denver hadn't liked the idea at first. There would be representatives there from the office of the first minister, and whatever she said was sure to get back to Clovinger.

"I understand," said Samara. "But there's always going to be time to grieve in your own way. This is our chance to make sure—"

Denver hadn't even looked up, but Samara could tell that she had just snapped back online by the tone of her voice. "Just do it." She cleared her throat and spoke more evenly. "Whatever you have to do. Just do it."

"I promise I'll speak as a friend, not as a politician."

She chuckled reflexively. "You know that's not what he'd want."

And so Samara began composing the eulogy.

The service itself felt like a nightmare, a sorrow beyond Samara's ability to fully take in. A reality too shattering to be real. Two hundred American refugees stood, dressed in the darkest clothes they'd been able to find in the donation piles, just outside the doors of the church, while the few Scots in attendance meandered in. This had been Samara's idea as well, to go in together as a group so that Denver would not have to walk down the aisle alone. When Denver arrived, arm-in-arm with Bristol, Samara gently signaled, and everyone walked through the doors and took their seats.

Denver's vacant face killed Samara, because she remembered the same reaction when her baby inside her had died. It had taken her months to return. She wondered how long it would be until Denver showed back up at her door with a bottle of wine and two plastic cups, if she ever would again.

Samara followed Denver and Bristol to the front pew, which had a dust-covered "reserved" sign hanging from it. She recognized people from Clovinger's office—a man and a woman—in the pew behind them, and nodded her head at them. They returned the nod but lowered their eyes when Denver turned her head to look.

There were photos—only photos, no holos—of him in frames covering a little table in front. Large candles on candlesticks that stood strong on the stone altar behind the table. With the intense candlelight behind them, the photos were shadowy, though the metal frames caught the light and shone. It gave the impression that his life had gone dark, that someone had turned out the lights to his life and not realized he was still in there.

The organ screamed on, finally settling on a resolving chord, and when the people were silent, Samara walked to the altar with her eulogy written on a piece of paper in her hands. Only when she heard the paper shaking did she realize she was trembling.

"Thank you all for coming to celebrate the life of Stephen Steiner. As most of you know, I'm Samara Shepherd, and I was privileged to call Stephen my close friend.

"Stephen was born in 2031 in a place that didn't have a name because the people there didn't think places needed names. We were raised to believe, as people who live there still believe—that our government had taken over the world and was ruling benevolently. For Stephen's entire childhood and adolescence, he believed he was being taken care of, despite being born a Four under our ranking system. His family was forced to work long hours for basic food rations and virtually no medicine. Because of the tight work schedules of Fours, his parents didn't see their son much, but Stephen always spoke highly of them and felt fortunate to have been raised in a loving home.

"Stephen befriended an Unregistered citizen during his job training, and his natural impulse toward empathy moved him to action. Two years into their friendship, he joined the Red Sea, a resistance group named after its benefactor, a charitable organization in the world he hadn't known existed. He worked for the Red Sea, helping Unregistered citizens escape to Canada until the Relocation.

"Stephen was very much in love with his wife, Denver. A story he loved to tell was how he was the only man in our country to choose his own wife. After seeing her profile, he was so smitten that he single-handedly hacked into the pairing database."

Some in the crowd gasped. Many chuckled. The man and woman behind Denver looked around at all of the people for whom arranged marriages had been the norm.

"He wasn't able to actually pair himself with her—though not for lack of trying—but he did manage to add himself to her candidates. And you need no better proof that they were meant to be. They were pair-ied and married, as we like to say. He helped his Unregistered brother-in-law escape the Relocation, and then escaped himself with his new wife. His bravery saved a family and created a new one."

Bristol reached his arm around his sister's shoulder. Denver raised a tissue to her eye and blotted.

"I can't say much here about the details of Stephen's role in bringing justice to our country or safety to our people. I can, however, say that he was a courageous, thoughtful man who loved to the point of hurt. No one knew the pain of compassion better than Stephen. He felt connected to others, and responsible for them. He entwined his destiny with the destiny of others. He was brave enough to fully open his heart to both the incredible beauty of the world—love, friendship, freedom—and the incredible horrors. I challenge all of us to take up his example and do the same."

After the service, Samara looked for a signal that she should follow Denver and Bristol back to the apartment they'd shared, up until a week ago, with Stephen. The siblings walked away from the church with low-hanging heads, deep in conversation, so Samara turned and walked the opposite way. Without thinking, she walked toward her favorite place in the city.

The bookshop had initially been a novelty. Back home, people projected words they wanted to read in their air on their watches, if they read at all. Reading for fun wasn't in vogue. When she'd first stumbled upon the shop, it had taken her multiple walks around the shelves to fully grasp what was actually happening here: there were books. They hadn't been destroyed. And, for just a bit of money, they could be hers.

Of course, she didn't have money, now or then. But she still loved to go and walk among the books and take in their scent.

She nodded to the owner, now a good friend. A stout little man with buttons always tugging apart in his mid-section, the owner lowered his head to look over his round black glasses and mouthed, "Are you okay?"

She nodded again, a little too vigorously, and then wandered toward the biographies.

One of Clovinger's own books was there on the little table. Samara put her fingers on the matte dustcover. Why had she never thought to read it before?

"That was beautiful."

Samara snapped to attention. Taye was standing on the other side of the table, looking at her intently.

"Taye? Oh my god!" Samara didn't know whether to laugh, cry, or run away. "What are you doing here? I haven't seen you in so long."

He was taller than she remembered, or maybe he was just standing a little taller. Once her good friend—though he'd wanted to be more than that—she'd lost track of him after he'd left Olympic Village to work, illegally, outside of London. A warehouse, if she remembered correctly.

"I heard about Stephen. You were great back there."

"You were at the funeral?"

"I was." He looked down and slid his hands into the pockets of his dated corduroys. "Do you want to take a walk?"

"Sure, I'd like to walk."

They found themselves moving toward Calton Hill, the park they frequented back when they'd first arrived here in Edinburgh and had nothing to do all day but wait. Samara was aware of their increasing proximity to St. Andrew's house, though she refused to acknowledge it out loud. She could be patient. She could wait for Clovinger's office to contact her. And anyway, Taye was busy talking about his own adventures.

"The guys are nice, but it's hard to hear them complain. All they do is complain all day long. It's too cold. Their back hurts. Their wives don't appreciate them. It never stops. I find myself keeping pretty quiet."

"I can't imagine that," said Samara with a laugh.

"It's hard to connect with people who taste sour in their vanilla lives. Sometimes I want to grab them by their shirts and tell them, 'Look, punk, my two brothers were treated as sub-human for the first five and eleven years of their lives! My parents are dead! I hid from a government that wanted me dead, and escaped across the ocean before they could find me!' Think about it—what would they say if I came out with that?"

Samara smiled and shook her head. "Maybe that you were trying to out-complain them."

"Exactly. Truth be told, it's not that bad at all. I come home feeling tired—a good tired—and then I get to sleep without being afraid some Metrics officer is going to rip my blankets off me."

"And where are you staying?"

"Well..." Taye dropped his gaze to the ground. "I met this girl."

"And you live with her?"

"I did, but no, not anymore." Taye crossed his arms in front of his chest and drew in a deep breath. "This is why I wanted to see you. I keep in touch with the guys from Olympic Village every now and then, you know, and—when they told me that someone had died trying to go back home, I was so afraid it was...I thought you might have..."

Samara's heart rose in her chest. This could not be happening again, not after everything she'd been through this week.

Taye blew the rest of his breath out of pursed lips and continued walking. "I'm moving back to Edinburgh, Samara. For good."

"Well, maybe not for good. We're still working on getting them to allow us to stay here."

"That's what I mean. I'm here to help you. I'm staying here."

They walked along in silence after that, breathing in the crisp spring air. Samara felt the heat of his hand next to hers more than once.

CHAPTER THIRTEEN

EVEN THOUGH BRISTOL HAD JUST GONE FOR A WALK THAT morning, he put a light jacket on in the afternoon too. He needed to get out of the apartment again.

For Bristol, Stephen's death created a black hole. Even though he was able to paint his mother after years of processing what it was like in that kitchen the moment she'd found that both of her children were gone, this was completely different. One day Stephen lived with them in this apartment, and the next, he did not. He never would again. The toothbrushes in the bathroom looked alone without Stephen's. Neither he nor his sister had gotten the hang of cooking for just two again yet. There were always leftovers, just enough for a plate for someone who wasn't there. His brother-in-law's brown boots, always by the door, were gone, and it seemed that they and everything else about Stephen had merely disappeared. Vanished. Vaporized into nothing.

That's how it was with his creativity, too. He'd been painting at a studio across town when Cindy called him on his watch—she was the only one who had his number—and told him what the aid workers at Olympic Village had told her. He'd put her on speaker so he was able to keep practicing, but when she told him that Stephen's plane had gone down, the brush dropped from his hand and he simply hadn't picked it back up. He sat there for a long time, staring at nothing, until finally he just left, the brush still on the floor and the canvas still set up.

He had created nothing for seven days. He ignored Cindy's calls.

In the park, life went on. Kids flew kites and couples ate ice cream. Bristol wished he was in the mood to reach out again to Samara and ask if she'd like to join him, but these haunting reminders of death were devastating and he didn't even really want to feel better. He thought about his father. About Nan and Lydia, the Red Sea volunteers in America who'd saved him. He thought of Stephen.

Bristol took a loop around the park and then took the long way back home. He approached a busy bridge that extended over a river and did a double take. There was someone under it with a hood over his head, scooting sideways on the balls of his feet, moving toward the center. From the top, no one would be able to see him, but Bristol was on the sidewalk just before the ramp.

"Hey!" he called to the person in the hoodie.

Jude turned to look back at him, his face streaked with tears.

"Jude?" asked Bristol.

"Don't try to stop me," said Jude, shouting to be heard above the traffic on the bridge. "It's my fault Stephen is dead. I know I can make myself do this, and I know I have to."

Bristol's pulse electrified. His breath became urgent; his body felt light. "Come back, Jude. It isn't your fault."

"It is! I gave us away!"

Bristol's mind asked, screaming, whether or not it could be true. He decided he didn't care. "Even if you did, your death won't bring him back."

"I'm the one who deserves this. He only wanted to help."

"Come back, Jude. This isn't going to make it right."

Jude let out a sob.

"Think of Samara," Bristol said quickly. "Think of Cork."

"I can't stop thinking about either of them." He turned to Bristol, the wind whipping his coarse curls away from his face. "They should both be free of me."

Bristol had always wondered, vaguely, if there was something wrong with Jude's head. Now that he was hanging in the air and talking nonsense, there was no doubt in his mind. He had no experience talking with the mentally unstable, so he tried talking to Jude like a small child.

"Jude," he said, dragging out the vowel. "Jude, there are lots of people who love you."

Jude sobbed again and lifted one of his hands to wipe his nose.

"Bye, Bristol," he said.

And he jumped.

Bristol jumped, too. The water felt like glass shattering when his body hit, then stabbed cold shards all over his skin. He hadn't really thought through the part after the jumping; Bristol could not swim. Even so, some survival instinct overtook him, and his arms and legs made swimming motions, pushing the water down so he could rise to the surface. When he made it to the air, he took a big breath, and then swore loudly. Water dripped from his forehead into his eyes, but he looked around for Jude.

He'd made it, too. He was only a few hundred feet away, making huge circles with his arms and breathing heavily. Bristol kicked his feet until his body started to move to Jude.

"Jude!" Bristol shouted. "Get over here!"

Jude swam towards Bristol with what looked like skilled technique.

"Get me to the shore," Bristol said, just before taking in a mouthful of dirty water.

Jude hooked one arm around Bristol's middle and swam, and

in moments, Bristol's legs found the floor of the river. He started to walk toward the pebble-lined shore, his legs heavy and his body freezing. "You! What were you thinking? Did you really think—"

Jude collapsed, folding himself so rapidly that his head nearly hit the brown rocks.

"Jude..."

"I just wanted to make things right!" he screamed. He flung a fist down, then did it again and again until blood flung from his awkward shape.

Bristol hunched with his hands on his knees until his breath slowed. He'd never been happier to hear it. He saw the blood coming from Jude's fleshy hand.

On the sidewalk, pedestrians slowed their pace and stared. More were crossing the street to have a look. Bristol imagined the sight through their eyes: two dark-skinned immigrants, soaking wet, both out of breath, one more emotional than the culture would ever allow. He grabbed Jude, still flailing his arms up and down, and dragged him onto the street. From there, he threw him over his shoulder and walked in the direction of his apartment. "Sorry!" he called to the people staring. "My brother! He fell, but we're fine now!"

Jude sobbed all the way to Bristol's apartment.

"What on earth!" said Denver when Bristol finally set Jude down in the doorway.

"Can you get us some towels?" asked Bristol and closed the door.

Denver darted in and out of the bathroom with her signature speediness, but it still gave Bristol a moment to realize she probably shouldn't be here when he talked to Jude. He took the towels from her and wrapped one around Jude's shoulders.

"Thanks. Can we have a moment?"

"No, you may not," she snapped. "This is my house too. What's going on?"

"Jude...fell in the river."

She glanced down at Jude's face, then back at Bristol. "Did he jump?"

Bristol sighed. "Yes."

"Because it's all my fault. I'm so sorry, but it's all my fault." Jude buried his face in his hands, and through his fingers, he told them everything.

CHAPTER FOURTEEN

Jude woke the next morning, still on Bristol and Denver's couch. He stared at the ceiling and thought of last night. After he'd admitted to blowing the mission and essentially killing Stephen, Denver had reacted much in the way he'd expected—lunging for his throat—but Bristol had restrained his sister and reminded her that Jude was probably out of his mind. Anything could have led to Stephen's plane being shot down.

Still, Jude was sick from shame and grief. At least someone knew now. If he couldn't kill himself, he at least had to suffer. Now, suffering meant that as many people knew of his failure as possible.

Jude turned to his side. Someone—probably Bristol; sure as hell not Denver—had covered him with a white knitted afghan. The weight of it had a grounding effect on Jude, and he felt his body melt down into the cushions.

Next to him, the doorknob jingled. He curled his body in tighter and pulled the afghan over his head.

Denver walked out of her room and opened the door. "Hey, Samara."

"Where is he?"

Denver's voice was cold. "There."

Jude cringed and felt the blanket being lifted away from him. Samara's face was close to him.

They stared at each other for a few moments. Jude braced himself for another assault, but Samara only stared until her bottom jaw began to tremble. Jude looked into her eyes and saw something he didn't expect—fear.

"Miss Shepherd..." He sat up and reached out. Samara hugged him. She was the only one who ever did that. He held onto her until silent tears trekked down his cheeks. His throat was too tight for air.

"I'm sorry," he said finally.

"I know."

"Tell him," said Denver, her feet planted and her arms crossed. "Tell him what he's done."

"Not now, Den."

"He needs to know."

"What?" asked Jude, his voice breaking.

Samara exhaled through her nose and lowered her eyes. "Parliament met last night at midnight. They voted to send us back."

Jude felt a stab in his stomach. "What? Doesn't the UC council have final authority?"

"They've withdrawn their support in light of the mission failure. Since they don't have a way forward with the mission now, they decided to let Scotland figure out what to do with us. And Scotland is going to send us back."

"When?"

"Soon," said Bristol, stepping out of his room. "I just talked to Cindy on the watch. She says the police will be by this afternoon to reclaim this apartment and to get all the essentials out this morning."

Things weren't quite coming together in Jude's mind. "They're sending us back? What does Daniel say?" Daniel was the coordinator at the Red Sea, the international aid group that initially provided support to the rebels in America. Surely he'd know what to do.

Samara rubbed the bridge of her nose. "The Red Sea is just an arm of the UC council. Daniel is trying to talk some sense into his superiors there, but it's not looking good." Samara's head dropped back, her throat exposed.

"There are only two hundred of us. Can't they just give us some manual labor and leave us alone?"

Samara made a sound that wasn't quite a laugh. "That's what I've been pushing, Jude, for years now. In the past, when the world's population was bigger, they may have overlooked two hundred people. Now they can't, or they won't."

"We'll have to go into hiding," said Bristol.

"Hiding," scoffed Denver. "And we thought we were done with that. Hiding."

"We're very lucky, actually," said Samara, directing her words at Jude. "As long as we leave before the police can apprehend us, the five of us can go to London."

"Five?"

"Well, seven, actually. Me, you, Denver, Bristol, Taye, and his two little brothers. Taye just came back to Edinburgh, but his employer in London said they'd take us at his warehouse, as long as we keep our heads down. It's a different one that he worked in; almost all of the workers at this one are not documented citizens. The conditions don't look great, but we're beggars now, not choosers. Taye had arranged it at first for just him and his brothers, but he thinks they'll take us too."

Cork was one of Taye's brothers. Jude hadn't spoken to him since their tense ride back from the airship.

"Are we ever going to get to—"

"No," said Denver. "No, we do not." She held up a hand to stop Samara from saying anything further. "No, we do not get to go home. No, we do not get to stay here. No, we do not get to live in peace. No, we do not get to feel safe. We're all on our own now. And we all have you to thank for that. All because you had to have your friend with you. What, are you in love with him or something?"

Jude blushed deeply.

"Oh my god." She stormed out of the room, and Bristol followed her.

Samara whisked the blanket up and folded it. "This could be useful," she said, "but it's so big."

"I can carry it," said Jude. "I don't have much." He knew the words would sound hollow, but he needed to say them anyway. "I'm sorry."

Samara put the blanket on Jude's lap. "I know you're sorry, Jude. I was angry at first, and part of me is still angry, but mostly I wouldn't want to feel the way you feel right now. We were in trouble before, you know? But I do wish we still had Stephen. He was our foundation."

Jude didn't say anything as they gathered a few more essential items and left the apartment to pack up at Olympic Village. He was pretty sure, though, that Samara had been the foundation. For him, she had always been the strongest person in his life—the one with answers amid chaos. It was a wonder she didn't know it.

CHAPTER FIFTEEN

SINCE THERE WERE NO SEATS ON THE TRAIN, DENVER THREW her overstuffed red tartan duffle bag on the floor and sat on it. She was aware of Bristol's gaze—a nonverbal warning not to draw attention—and ignored it, huffing loudly while she leaned back against the wall.

Ten days. Stephen and stupid Jude were only supposed to be gone for ten days, and then their fate would have been in the steady hands of professional spies and military fighters. Now those same professionals had turned on them. If they saw someone following too close or a person in uniform, they'd have to find a way to dodge them.

Bristol flinched, a tiny gesture that anyone else may have missed. But not Denver.

"It takes some getting used to," she said.

He crouched next to her, and she could smell aftershave. He must have made sure to put some on, not knowing when his next shower would be. "What?"

"Not wearing a watch."

Bristol bit his lip. "It didn't take that long to get used to having it on; it can't take that long to readjust."

"It shouldn't, but it does. They're so cleverly designed; they feel like an extension of yourself after an hour. The loss of it makes you realize how vulnerable you are."

Bristol made circles on his wrist with his thumb. "Good thing I'm adaptable."

"A family trait." Samara crouched on the floor next to them. Jude, Taye, Cork, and Henry joined them until they formed a little circle.

"So, when are we going to talk about the important stuff?" asked Taye, looking at Samara.

Bristol's heart constricted. If this wasn't enough of a nightmare, of course Taye had come back and immediately begun sniffing around Samara. He'd briefly considered going back to Cindy and asking if she knew of any way his fame could protect him—but he didn't want to end up married to her, so he'd left without saying goodbye.

"What's that?" asked Samara.

"We're running again. A week ago, there was a plan in place to stop running for good. How can we get it going again?" Taye asked.

"You're one to talk." Bristol was surprised to hear a growl in his voice, but he tried not to let it show. "You ran from the running."

"Ha! I like to think of it as moving onto better opportunities."

"Better than liberating our home? Better than rescuing our families and friends?" Bristol asked. Denver put a hand on his shoulder.

Taye flipped his hand. "Says the hardened revolutionary who drew pictures for the resistance."

Bristol jumped to his feet; Taye did the same, half a second behind. "I never liked you," said Bristol, clenching his fists at his sides.

Samara stood and whispered harshly, "People are watching."

The two men sat, both eyeing each other over crossed arms.

"The whole world is watching," said Taye. "Which brings me back to my original point." He turned his chin up at Samara. "What are we going to do?"

"Nurse Sue and Marty May are on a fishing ship to Norway. Kareale and Danovan should be in Ireland by now. People are scattering as far as Poland and Austria. How are we supposed to coordinate now?"

"Samara's right," said Denver. "The best we can hope for at this point is a life where no one bothers us. I'm willing to keep my head down if it means a little bit of peace."

"That's all it will be," said Jude quietly.

Bristol looked up at him. In his peripheral, he saw Denver's jaw tighten. "Excuse me?" she asked.

"A little bit of peace. Just for us, and it'll never be for certain. Back at the monastery, someone said—" Jude bowed his head as if he didn't know whose gaze to avoid. "Someone told us that if we were good at accepting defeat, we wouldn't be here. Wouldn't be alive, really."

Bristol closed his eyes and felt the train jerk underneath him. No one spoke as it gathered speed and volume. He supposed that even though Jude had been the one to muck everything up for everyone he loved, he was, in a sense, family. He was stuck with him. And even though he knew that Jude was the last person he should be listening to, he had a point.

Samara, of course, was the one to break the silence. "You know...the opposite of a little bit of peace is an abundance of conflict."

"Well," said Denver, looking daggers at Jude, "what else have we got to lose?"

Bristol and the others were allowed to drop their things off in their room before immediately being put to work. Bristol was afraid that all of their things wouldn't fit in one room, and was reminded to once again lower his standards when he saw it. Just a small room with blankets and sleeping bags in muted colors strewn about in no order. There were no windows along the white cinderblock walls. It smelled strongly of mold.

"Here," said the foreman, shoving an ancient handheld electronic device into Bristol's hand. It was gray and about the length of his hand, with a screen on top and numbered buttons below it. "When an order comes in, this will beep. The number of the bin will show up here. Go get it, and put it here on the conveyer belt for shipping."

They worked for nearly eight hours after their ten-hour train ride. By the time they made it back to their moldy room, Bristol fell asleep without even unpacking his own sleeping bag. He slept beside Samara on the cold tile floor. Just before he fell asleep, he wondered who might be on her other side.

CHAPTER SIXTEEN

SAMARA SPLASHED SOME WATER ON HER FACE IN THE SINK THAT stood in the corner of the room they all slept in. She knew she'd regret not brushing her teeth, but she was already late and being fired was unimaginable. She rushed out the door and down the metal-grid steps to the warehouse floor below.

It wasn't that they weren't eager to formulate a new plan to infiltrate America with no financial or intelligent support from any government agencies. It was just that there didn't seem to be any time to do it.

She had forgotten what it had been like to work like this: every waking hour, eating as fast as she could in order to spend more time working. She hadn't spoken to anyone longer than three consecutive minutes since they'd arrived two weeks ago and, to make matters worse, every time they did speak, it was about fetching things and dropping them off again. She couldn't seem to get away from it.

She was disappointed in herself for feeling so above it all. After all, she was raised a Five, and jobs like this one was what she'd expected to do for her entire life before Metrics surprised her with the assignment of Education Manager. This was the kind of job her parents would consider respectable. Not fancy, certainly, but honest, with a chance to keep physical strength and stamina up, and the ability to keep herself fed without taking any handouts.

Samara's shoulders and neck ached, and she tried once again to put the pain out of her mind. Taye, coming from behind her, quickened his pace and handed her a handheld scanner.

"Here," he said. "I've already gotten your first order for you."

"You're a lifesaver. I overslept."

"I'm sorry. I would have made sure you were up. Who was the last person out of the room? Why didn't they make sure you were awake?"

Samara wasn't quite sure, but she thought it might have been Bristol. She vaguely remembered shutting him out with the blanket over her head, insisting she'd be up in one minute.

"I don't remember."

"I'll speak with everybody. We need to stick together. If one of us is out, there's nowhere for us to go."

"I could always join Nurse Sue in Norway."

"Not possible."

"I was joking."

"I'm not." Taye stopped and took a precious few seconds to take her free hand. "I need us to all take care of each other for one reason and one reason only. I don't know what the next step from here is, but I know I want to take it with you."

Samara really wished she'd brushed her teeth. She pressed her lips together and looked over his ear. "Let's just get through today. Thank you for covering for me."

She broke away and walked toward the bins of sex toys. One out of every three orders seemed to come from that area, so it was a good guess. Her scanner buzzed. She was right.

"What was that?" asked Denver, retrieving an unwrapped dildo and already starting off.

Samara grabbed a box of edible underwear, though she wasn't exactly sure it was the correct flavor specified on the screen, and caught up with her. "Nothing. He wants us all to be more collaborative."

"Is that what we're calling it now? Collaboration?"

"He has a crush on me. So what?"

"So, you're enjoying the attention at the expense of my brother."

Samara's face flashed hot. "No, I'm not."

Denver shot her an eyebrows-up look and tossed her dildo onto the conveyer belt for shipping.

Samara threw her box on the belt and seethed. Attention was the last thing she wanted. She wanted time and space to think. Why was everyone so insistent on love? When they'd first arrived in Edinburgh, Bristol had wanted to marry her that first week, without any thoughts of their security. They hadn't yet spent a month as foreign runaways and Taye was already making declarations of love and public displays of affection. Denver should be less worried about emotional affairs and more worried about having a funeral with no body, as they had for her husband just a few weeks ago. Having no time to think, plan, or strategize pissed her off enough, but having precious mental energy stolen by matters of the heart infuriated her.

All day long she worked, shoulders knotting up further from her anger, vision blurred by fury. She grabbed another box of anal plugs and threw them down on the belt, hoping whoever was wasting money on that crap would get one stuck and have to explain their dilemma to the emergency room doctors. What a good use of public dollars that would be. No, but keeping refugees would just be too costly.

"Miss?" the foreman asked softly.

Samara startled. Why had he gotten so close?

"Miss, can I see you in my office, please?"

"Oh—of course."

She followed him up the stairs, and Taye and Bristol craned their necks from the floor to watch them ascend.

The foreman was a short man, about the same height as

Samara, with hairy arms and a bald patch on the crown of his head.
He wore a red plaid shirt with the sleeves rolled up that cut into
his thick forearms. He was sweating more than anyone Samara had
ever seen before.

"Been a lot of mistakes lately."

"Excuse me?" Samara asked. She genuinely wasn't sure whether
he meant on the floor or, as his expression would suggest, in his
personal life.

"Mistakes. I've had to resubmit most of your orders out today.
And it isn't just today, either!"

Samara began to say something, then closed her mouth. She
knew she'd been sloppy for the past few hours, but before today,
she'd double checked every order to make sure it was right. *Please*,
she thought, *please give me a warning*.

"I've got a...problem myself," he said. The sweat all over his
face gave him the illusion of a glow under the florescent lights. He
twisted the rod to shut the venetian blinds that overlooked the
warehouse floor.

Inside, something told Samara to run. Samara told that
something to shut up. She had run far and long enough. It was
time to stand up, not shrink away.

The foreman stepped close to Samara and grabbed her hand.
She tried to pull away, but before she could, he was rubbing it
against his trousers. "There's my problem," he said. "If you'd just
help me with this, I'd overlook your laziness."

She jerked her hand back and gnashed her teeth. "Who do you
think you are?"

"Me?" He laughed, but Samara knew fear when she heard it.
"I'm a bloke who is saving your ass, that's who I am! You'd be going
back to die if it weren't for me! And what have I asked for?
Nothing!"

"You've asked for plenty. And you're not getting any more."

He stepped in again, this time with an unhinged gleam in his
eyes, and took her hand. This time, he bent back her wrist toward

her forearm until it trembled and threatened to break under the stress. She cried out, but he put his fleshy hand over her mouth.

He whipped her around until his face was in her hair, next to her ear. "Now, I'm sorry about that. I didn't want to do that. You made me mad."

Samara bit him, sinking her teeth into the fleshy part of his hand under his pinky finger. He bellowed out in pain and threw her onto the floor. She very nearly froze in fear, but the extra second he took to check if his hand was bleeding was all she needed to bolt to the door. She was all the way down the stairs before she drew another breath.

CHAPTER SEVENTEEN

Though all of the others had tucked themselves into the various nests of blankets in the dark that night, Bristol stood at the door like a centurion. Samara had followed the foreman into his office and, moments later, had shot out like a tiger from its cage.

Whatever had happened in there, Bristol was sure they were no longer safe.

He pressed his fingertips into his forehead and massaged at his headache. Inside, his head throbbed with something more than pain. It was an internal warning. He recognized it as the voice that accompanied him back when he'd sneak out at night to go paint, alerting him to danger.

He heard her footsteps, the careful cadence of her gait before he heard the doorknob turn. He touched her arm in the dark. She hissed and jerked away. Bristol's breath rose into his upper chest and stayed there, slow but shallow.

"What happened?" asked Bristol.

"Nothing."

"We need to leave again."

"I can handle this," said Samara, her shoulders hunching in toward each other. "We are not leaving again."

"Ha! First of all, you're out of your mind if you think we'd let you handle this on your own," said Denver, sitting up from her sleeping bag. Jude, Taye, Cork, and Henry rose from their blankets. Taye pulled the cord hanging from the center of the ceiling and the naked lightbulb above lit up the room. "Second, you're absolutely right. We are not leaving again."

"What's the plan, Den?" asked Taye.

Denver side-eyed him, but continued. "I think I can get my hands on some poison. And once I do, I think I can make sure he takes it."

Bristol crossed his arms. "You would not."

"Let's try and see, little brother."

"Do you know how much more trouble we'd be in if they thought we'd killed someone?"

"We're not going to get caught." Denver said.

"How?"

"There are lots of other workers here. They'd never be able to prove it was us."

"There are security cameras on the floor. They'd narrow it down."

"Even if they couldn't," said Jude, "we're not taking the chance that one of them could get locked up because of us."

"Fine," said Denver. "Fine. So an asshole thinks he has a little power and decides to beat us up." Denver gave Samara a look, one that Bristol was familiar with. It was the look Denver gave when she knew there was more to a story, but she wasn't in a good place to ask. Bristol had seen it many times over the breakfast table back home when she'd asked, in front of Mom, how he slept last night. "Does he just get to walk away?"

"Yes," mumbled Samara.

"No," said Jude. "I have an idea."

Denver snorted through her nose. "Whatever it is, we're not doing it. Your idea days are done."

"Let's just go to sleep," Samara said.

"At his age, he's not doing illegal things for the first time. He hired us! That's illegal. There must be more." Jude stood firm on his feet. "He wears a watch. Let's take it to the police."

"You can't just take someone's watch to the police." Bristol knew he needed to talk Jude down in order to shield him from Denver—and Denver from herself. "They're busy people. If we had a claim and proof, that might be something."

"He's not doing illegal things for the first time..." said Samara. Bristol watched as her eyes went from vacant to bright. "Jude, that's great idea. We need to organize."

"Organize what?" asked Taye.

"Wrong question."

Taye grinned. "Organize who?"

"The other women he's attacked."

Bristol's breath froze in his throat.

CHAPTER EIGHTEEN

DENVER CREPT DOWN THE CATWALK TO THE ROOM WHERE TEN other women slept in the dead of night. Over the past few days, they'd talked to some others who were in the same situation as Samara, and tonight would be their first meeting with all of them there. Denver's poison idea turned out to be quite popular among the club that no one wanted to be in, but no one expressed interest in wanting to deliver it personally. Denver insisted she didn't mind, but Bristol had talked her out of it.

At first, the women that Denver and Samara had approached seemed reluctant to talk, and many insisted they didn't have time. Denver was learning, though, that people always made time for what was important to them. Before it had been sleep. Now, above all, it was making sure the smelly man with the sickening sense of entitlement was brought to justice one way or another.

The moment Denver and Samara entered the room, all of the women began speaking at once.

"He told her that he'd deport me if I didn't—"

"He grabbed my hair and shoved me down on the—"

"I haven't been able to look at my husband since—"

"—me too!"

As much as Denver wanted to get on with the details of how they'd bring their monster down, she stopped to listen to every story. Most of the women were in the country illegally, fleeing other unsafe countries. The stories were all similar in both tone and content: the foreman had called them into his office, told them something along the lines of "you owe me" or "you messed up."

They were unified on their problems and the desire to bring him to justice, but there was no consensus on how.

"We can't go to the police, since most of us are here illegally. We could try homespun justice, but if we got caught, the risk of being deported isn't worth it," Denver reiterated.

Samara was being too quiet. Denver wasn't used to working alone—she needed a partner. They needed to overthrow this foreman as soon as possible so Samara could start healing and she could have her partner back. Stephen would never be back, she knew, but at least there was a chance with Samara. Even if she'd never be the same, at least she'd be there.

The other women slowly transitioned from offering their ideas on how to move forward to retelling their stories. Denver was going to try to redirect them, but stopped when she saw Samara's face. She was clearly taking it all in, nodding and drawing breath as if she was waiting her turn to say what exactly had happened to her. In this room, Denver was the immensely fortunate one. Even though the man she loved was dead, most all of her sexual experiences had been reciprocal, both trying to fill each other up. She'd never been emptied and cast aside. It seemed to her that through these retellings, these women were attempting to re-right themselves.

"We should write these down," said Denver after more than an hour of listening. "And send them out."

Samara lifted her chin slightly. "In the packages?"

"Yes."

"The police will come," said one of the women with a tremble in her voice.

"One of us can watch for them. There are more than enough of us to share work to cover for one or two missing workers. We'll hide when they come, then when another foreman comes, we can work until…"

"Until when?" asked Samara.

Denver sighed. "Hopefully there'll be a lull between this jerk leaving and another one coming. That may give us enough time to come up with our next move."

Denver woke a few mornings later with a folded letter in her bra. Most of the women were not comfortable writing the stories themselves, so Samara and Denver did interviews and wrote them all. They all ended the same way: *if you receive this and want to help, please call the police at 8 p.m. and tell them to go immediately to 1700 Industrial Avenue…*

She knew it would be fine to just fold it twice, but she'd opted to keep folding until it was a tiny square, in case the foreman heard crinkling and grew suspicious. She knew he wouldn't, but she couldn't shake the habit. She was far away from anyone caring so much about control. In a way, this guy was the perfect target. He had, for years, gotten away with heinous behavior. He never expected a consequence. Not from these invisible women.

They'd agreed that the first same-day package they sent of the day would have the letters inside. Denver's letter held a copied version of Samara's story. Samara had handed it to her, and Denver had simply folded it up, unread. If Samara wanted her to know, eventually she would tell her.

The other women caught their eyes in subtle fractions of seconds to communicate that they had mailed their letter. The rest of the day continued as usual. The concrete floor pounding against Denver's feet, the rough cardboard irritating her fingers, the shrieks of the forklift amplified in the open space.

Seven o'clock came. Bristol, charged with watch, signaled

through the chain that there were no signs of police from the roof.
That was good, Denver thought. Whoever had read their letters
had followed instructions. Her upper lip was still wet with sweat.

The energy in the giant room changed as eight o'clock grew
closer. People looked longer in her face, and the overall pace,
which usually slowed a bit as the day waned into evening, grew
faster and more frantic.

The foreman didn't seem to notice.

Orders kept coming in, and Denver's mind swung wildly from
fear to fear. What if no one had called? What if the police had
decided not to come? As dire as things were, Denver thought it
would be worse if the women here were ignored. Their suffering
had been silent for too long.

Eight o'clock came. Went. Orders came in and out. Feet hurt.
Fingers burned. Ears ached. The same as every night.

At ten, the whistle blew. Once again, Denver untied the canvas
apron from her waist and hung it on a worn peg on the wall.

"What do you think happened?" whispered Samara from the
neighboring peg.

"I don't know," said Denver. "But I'm afraid that—"

Jude ran to them. "They're coming," he said under his breath,
then continued speed-walking down the line with his warning.

Denver and Samara wasted no time. Together with the other
women, they walked out the back door and climbed into the
dumpster. Since yesterday was trash day, it easily accommodated all
ten of them. Denver stood beside it and offered her basketed
hands to boost everyone climbing inside. As she catapulted Samara
into the dumpster, she heard the police man shouting inside. *Please
don't let them check their citizenship status*, she prayed before jumping
for Samara's outstretched arms above.

Inside, just one level of trash bags broke her fall. The bags
squished under her as she found her feet. Though the stench
weighed heavy against her and threatened to overpower her senses,
she opened her mouth to breathe and pressed her ear against the
cold, rusted metal.

No one else made a move. They only looked to her. Denver wished Samara would, but she seemed to be more comfortable looking to Denver leading her out this time.

"Sounds like they got him," Denver whispered to the group. "But if no one's come to get us yet, they must be still inside..."

She listened hard and heard a car door slam and what sounded like a fleet of cars driving away. No sirens, which she was glad of—there hadn't been a struggle. But no one came for them.

"Should we go check?" asked Samara.

"No," said Denver. "This is what we all agreed on. Someone will come, I know—"

"What if they've checked the boys' citizenship status?" asked one of the women whose teenage son was inside. "We should go and see if they're okay."

"I can still hear voices," said Denver. She hadn't heard a voice since the cars had driven away, but she needed to maintain control for everyone's safety. She remembered Metrics officials, lying to them all of their lives, for largely the same reason, and shuddered. "Let's wait at least an hour."

They waited for what felt like two.

Finally, the door squealed and the dumpster rang with a coded knock: once, then twice. Everyone inside, Denver included, breathed audibly, no longer able to smell the garbage, overcome with relief.

Denver climbed to the top and poked her head over the edge. "All clear, little brother?"

Bristol put his hands on his hips. "All clear, sis."

Jude, Taye, Cork, Henry, and a dozen others came out to help the women out of the dumpster and onto the ground. Denver took in fresh air, glad to be filling both lungs with air that wasn't rotten.

"Well," said Taye, his voice booming with charisma, "they did it! Hip, hip!"

"Hooray!" shouted every male voice. The women were quiet, but Denver couldn't stop her smile, especially when Samara reached for her hand and squeezed.

CHAPTER NINETEEN

SINCE NO ONE HAD INFORMED THE MANAGEMENT TEAM THAT one of their foremen had been arrested, Jude and the others enjoyed a morning off. The second foreman wouldn't arrive until noon, and when he did, he would find a few dozen warehouse workers dressed and ready to work, innocently awaiting one of their betters to come unlock the technology cabinet where the scanners were kept.

Jude slept until the sun had been up for hours. He dressed in his blue jumpsuit, extraordinarily similar to the orange one he'd worn while in Fox County Juvenile Detention Center, and headed downstairs, where Samara, Bristol, and Denver were already in their aprons, sitting huddled on the cement floor.

Bristol handed him an energy bar. Normally, they ate these in giant bites, as fast as they could, while running to fetch the next order. Today, Jude actually tasted it. It tasted completely different than he'd expected—nutty and fruity and not altogether half bad. Though probably because of the way his body was used to consuming it, it still had the same stomach-turning affect.

"It can't be that different," said Denver, looking at Bristol.

"What can't be?" asked Jude.

Denver and Bristol laughed. Samara looked over her shoulder, an outline of a smile on her face that didn't seem to come from within. Denver re-crossed her legs on the floor. "When Bristol and I were little, we made a little city in the sewer."

Jude recoiled. "In the what?"

"I know. So gross. But it was right before they separated out the Unregistered from the rest of us in school—right before we got our watches. Bristol and the other neighborhood kids and I would crawl down under the street and play. It was pretty dirty down there—"

"It was a sewer," said Bristol.

"Uh-huh, but it was where we wanted to play. There were cameras at the park, and we were about to get personal surveillance for the rest of our lives, so the sewer it was. We organized a group of the little neighbor kids and we all cleaned it up together."

Bristol laughed. "We made the kids shut up while we cleaned, and in return, everyone got a turn to hang from the manhole."

"While the rest of us made a soft landing for them down below."

Jude turned the empty wrapper over in his hand. He'd never noticed the matte texture of the paper before. "Trading social interaction for productivity? A small personal reward at the expense of all workers? Reminds me of Metrics."

Denver nodded. "We could see what about their operation worked, even as children. We exploited it."

Bristol chuckled. "And we got that sewer as clean as a whistle."

"Before the next day, when it turned into a sewer again."

"Reminds me even more of Metrics."

"What's your point?" asked Jude, interrupting the two siblings.

"We think we can run this place," said Denver. "With a few efficiency tips picked up from home sweet home, we could work fewer hours on shipping so we can focus on the real problem. The owner of this warehouse is going to come in today. When he does, I'll be ready to present my ideas on how to maximize efficiency for him. What he won't know—what he doesn't need to know—is how we'll be spending the free time he's about to give us."

"We still can, right?" Jude asked.

"Still can what?" asked Denver. She seemed to be in a much better mood after her victory last night. Even Samara raised her eyebrows, a brief glimpse of her usual perky self.

"We can still liberate the United States. We can undo what's been done."

They looked at each other. Bristol was the first to smile. "We think so," he said.

"It has to be us," said Denver, looking hard into Jude's face, her features solid stone. "We have to be the ones to go make initial contact with the Bird. I won't be able to construct identities as solid as Stephen's team was able to, but I've got the blueprints. And being higher-ranked tiers, we know how to interact with the people who'll make the decisions to let us through."

"You and me? We're going to see the Bird? The crazy old man?"

"The one who helped develop the tier system. The one who believes it's possible to dismantle Metrics. Making contact with him was part of Stephen's mission. I don't suppose he shared that with you," said Denver with an edge in her voice. "My husband was a smart man."

"I won't make mistakes this time."

"Do us one better," said Denver. "Make smarter mistakes. Ones that can help us survive."

Jude nodded, unable to meet her eye.

"First step for you and I," said Bristol, nodding his head at Jude, "is going back to Edinburgh, by way of London."

"What's back in Edinburgh?"

Bristol's lips stiffened. "And old friend."

Samara picked at her cuticles.

While Denver made her case to the warehouse owner, Bristol and

Jude unbuttoned their jumpsuits and packed their bags. Jude pulled his careworn cherry-colored hoodie over his head, but Bristol asked him to wear one of his muted-toned jackets over it to attract less attention. The red hood still stuck out against the olive-green zip-up, Bristol worried, so he tucked it inside the back of the jacket. Jude stood still while he did and remembered how much he'd basked in these small moments of concern when they all first found each other—his adopted older siblings and himself.

"Ready?" asked Bristol.

Jude nodded, but he didn't feel ready at all. They walked out of the doors of the warehouse for the first time in weeks. He bowed his head in preparation for the wind, which lashed at his hairline. Spring in the UK retained much more of a chill than back home, but he was beginning to get used to it.

They walked down the paved road, with identical warehouses flanking either side.

"Let's try this one," said Bristol.

Both of them looked over their shoulders and jogged to the far side of the large sheet metal building to the truck yard. Most of them were already loaded with shipping containers, but there was one smaller truck with an open bed. The inside was soiled with chicken feces. Bristol looked at Jude, nodded, and climbed inside. He extended his hand to help Jude up.

They huddled toward the back, where they were partially covered.

"What now?" asked Jude.

"Denver was up all night studying the shipment patterns. She thinks these trucks go out to collect the live animals around midday. They go in—" Bristol pointed to the building "—and then they go out in those refrigeration trucks." He shuddered. "Be glad we don't have to travel in one of those."

Jude nodded. They waited, Jude playing with the fragments of words he saw on the side of the other trucks. He made as many new words and sounds he could of "reliable," "fresh," and "poultry."

Finally, a man approached the truck, yelling something to another man staying behind. Jude and Bristol froze. He switched his breathing to shallow sips of air. *Please, please don't check the back.*

The man didn't. He barked a laugh and started the ignition, backing the vehicle up with such force that Bristol was launched forward on his hands. Jude winced at the noise he made, but the driver still didn't bother to check his cargo bed. Together, Bristol and Jude watched the gray warehouses fly by on the road.

Jude noticed Bristol's lips moving. "What?" he asked.

"I'm not talking to you," Bristol said low in his ear.

"You're talking to yourself?" asked Jude, suddenly concerned.

"No," said Bristol. "I'm just...*hoping* that Denver is successful and Samara is safe and Taye finds something new to do with his life."

"Oh," said Jude. "You're praying."

"Praying seems to mean that you think something is taking care of you," said Bristol. "I'm not so sure about that. I guess I'm...wishing."

If something wasn't looking after them, Jude thought, *they were the luckiest humans in history.*

The truck slowed as traffic increased.

"We need to jump soon," said Bristol.

"London is still twenty kilometers away," said Jude.

"This may be the closest we get. This truck isn't going into the city, remember. And there are no cars behind us now."

Jude found his feet, but kept his knees bent to maintain his balance. "I'm ready."

They walked to the edge of the bed, where the road flew beneath them like a river. Jude was reminded of how he had tried to end it all only a few weeks ago and how much easier it was back then when he was soaked with guilt and drained of hope. Now, he considered his hesitation an indication that he was getting healthier. If Bristol wasn't going to pray, Jude thought, then he would. He squeezed his eyes shut. He jumped.

CHAPTER TWENTY

SAMARA SCRUBBED AT HER FACE WITH THE WASHCLOTH THE NEXT morning. It wasn't nearly abrasive enough, but she tried to compensate by digging her fingernails into her skin under the fabric and making small circles on her temples, cheekbones, and jawline. When she was done, her skin shone ruddy in the mirror and she felt worse than ever. At least Bristol was gone and wouldn't see her. Couldn't ever see her like this again. She moved over the toilet for a moment, wondering whether her body would spontaneously vomit again, as it had several times over the past few days.

Only dry heaves. Samara leaned against a wall for support and talked herself down again. You're here. He's not. The more she tried to convince herself that she was the winner, the more her brain pulled her down the sinkhole of despair. What if he comes back? What if he's angry? What if Denver fails? She lunged for the toilet and threw up bits of energy bar from last night's dinner.

Samara raised her head only when she heard a knock on the bathroom door. *Please be Denver,* Samara thought. "Come in."

Taye opened the door an inch and spoke from the other side. "Samara?"

Samara lowered her head back into the bowl. "What?"

"I, um...have your scanner. We're about ready to start again. I haven't talked to Denver yet, but it seems like they liked whatever she had to say. The orders have been piling up, so it's going to be a busy evening. We'll probably work into the night."

Samara felt broken all over. There was no part of her, internal or external, that felt unaffected. She hated Taye for reminding her of the inevitable. She hated the world for going on creating more work and refusing her rest and recovery. But what to do? Though she wanted nothing more than to stick his head down this miserable toilet, he was right—there was work to be done.

"Coming."

She dragged herself up off the slimy tile and wiped her mouth with the back of her hand. Just as she found her feet, she heard Denver's voice from the hallway. "What are you doing in there?"

"Samara's in there," answered Taye.

"Then you have even less of a reason to be in there," said Denver. "Give me her scanner. They need you down on the floor."

Taye left wordlessly, but Denver stayed, swinging open the door and rushing inside. She took Samara's arm. "Let's get you back in bed. I layered a bunch of blankets, so it should be more comfortable. And I took *Great Expectations* before Jude left, so it's there if you want it."

"What? Taye just said that we'd have to work all night."

"We'll work until bed tonight, just to catch up. But you have the day off."

"I don't think I should—"

"You are taking the day off. The week if you need it." Denver leveled her nose to Samara's and spoke uncharacteristically slowly. "When I lost Zion, all I wanted to do was to have some time to stop being productive. I was completely drained, and it was unbearable to think of siphoning more energy away. I needed it, but I didn't get it. I was with people who didn't understand what it meant to miscarry."

Samara's face pounded with the sudden rush of blood. "I am so sorry."

Denver clicked her tongue and led Samara out of the bathroom. "If you're sorry, go to bed. Think, read, cry, and sleep. Stare at the wall for an hour. It'll make us both feel better."

Samara did nothing else all day but read, think, cry, and sleep, in that order, over and over again, as Denver had instructed. When darkness fell, she reallocated the blankets around the room again to make places for the others to sleep. Taye, Henry, and Cork came in and talked a bit about the orders and how nice it was to work for themselves. They did not talk about the next steps to return to the United States. Samara pretended to be asleep.

Long after the first snores from the boys had broken the silence of the room, Denver walked in. The familiar crackle made Samara cringe.

"No thank you," Samara told Denver.

"You need to eat."

"I'll just throw it up again."

"Water then?"

Samara sat up. "Fine."

"It's warm. I found a slice of lemon in the fridge."

Samara wrapped her hands around the Styrofoam cup and brought it to her lips. "You would have made a great mom," she said. No sooner had the words escaped her mouth than she wished she would have stopped herself. "I'm sorry."

"You're so sorry," said Denver and folded her arms around her knees. She sighed. "Thank you. That does mean a lot." She paused, and Denver got the feeling she wanted to touch her somehow but was restraining herself. "Are you okay?"

"No."

"Good. You should take some time to be decidedly not okay after what that asshole did." Denver scratched the back of her head, skewing her short hair. "He'll be in jail a while. No one is posting bond."

Samara nodded. "Have you heard from Bristol or Jude?"

"No. But I watched the truck pull out. They should have been on it. They're probably in London by now."

Samara stared into space while Denver tactfully left her to get ready for bed. She almost wished they had discussed Bristol going back to Cindy before she'd been attacked. She longed for the emotional capacity to care whether or not she'd lose him forever. It seemed amazing that there was even a time she cared whether or not she'd lose him for a few months, or that she'd be jealous that another woman would be Bristol's wife for a short time, or forever. Now, Samara was broken in a way unique to every other way she'd been broken before. Her very core was cracked, her trust gone forever. Sleeping in a room with other people, even people she had trusted before, seemed much too dangerous. She pulled on a jacket, one of Bristol's old ones that he'd given to her. It had been in her possession so long that most days she forgot that it had been his at all. But tonight, the thick fleece felt protective and warm, perfect for a little walk.

She only made it a few steps under that heavy fleece before she realized she could not walk by herself. What was she thinking? The foreman was no longer here, it was true, but there were other men here that were no longer supervised. And what the women had done hadn't exactly been fierce. They'd needed the support of the other men. What if one of them attacked Samara tonight? She turned back to the door, but she'd only walk right into the problem of not wanting to sleep with others around.

Without good reasons not to move in one direction or another, she put her back to the wall and sank down. She rested her cheekbones on her knees. She wouldn't close her eyes.

Denver stole into the hallway and crouched down beside Samara.

"Talk," she said.

But Samara couldn't talk. Even if she did have something she wanted to say, the mere thought of forcing air from her lungs to her throat to make her vocal chords vibrate required more effort than she could exert. Besides, she couldn't possibly talk about what had happened to her out loud. If she said the words, then the air from her lungs would give them a kind of life, and what had happened would be real. If she spoke, she'd have to figure out what to do next.

Denver sighed, and the two sat in silence for several long minutes. Finally, Denver squeezed the bridge of her nose.

"He'll only marry her for the green card. And that's only if she agrees. He's promised not to mislead her and be totally honest about the reasoning. He even told me he'd let her know that he has feelings for you."

"I feel terrible that he has feelings for me," said Samara, her eyes not focused on anything in particular but still frozen in place. "I can't do anything about them. I can't be with him."

"Not right now, but some day."

"Not ever."

"You'll heal. It won't happen overnight."

"You don't know what it's like."

"I've never been hurt like you, but I'm not a stranger to pain. And I know that it'll do no good to insist that you'll never feel better. You won't ever feel the same, but you'll feel better than you do right now."

Nodding seemed like the best answer. Samara wasn't sure if she wanted Denver to stay or go.

Denver sighed, planted her feet, and rose. She left and came back with two blankets and pillows. She wedged hers behind her back and leaned against the wall. Samara took in the sight of Denver, her eyes closed, her own future as uncertain as hers. Maybe she had a point. She was, after all, still here.

CHAPTER TWENTY-ONE

BRISTOL OPENED THE DOOR TO THE DINGY YOUTH HOSTEL FOR Jude. They figured the best place to hide for a while would be a place where people of all nationalities came and went, too busy with the adventures of their own lives to be nosy about anyone else's. He'd used most of his remaining money to buy fake passports for himself and for Jude, but he wouldn't count on them to get them out of the UK. Though they'd been good enough for the overgrown children running the youth hostel, he knew they wouldn't fool a customs official.

The young man at the front desk had barely glanced at the fake passports.

"Canada, eh? Bloody brilliant," he'd said, nodding his head enthusiastically to a rhythm only he seemed to be able to hear.

Bristol was better at concealing and omitting than he was at lying, so he stayed silent. Jude too. The young man frowned.

"You don't seem like the kind of Canadians I've met, though," he said, and for a moment glanced down at the passports in his hands.

"Oh, you've been to Canada?" asked Bristol, hoping to shift the focus. "Where?"

"Yeah, mate! Toronto. First class weed in that city, man. Top notch."

"We've never been. We're from Edmonton," said Jude.

"Never heard of it," said the man, moving the long blond strands out of his eyes and properly looking at their passports now.

Shit. Bristol walked away from the desk, examining the Tibetan prayer flags hanging from the doorway, but Jude pointed to a map on the wall behind a desk.

"It's the capitol of Alberta. West. It's very cold there, and we don't get out much."

"I feel that. I feel that. You're the first cats I've met from Alberta, then! Welcome to London!" He handed the fake passports back and showed them to their room.

This room also housed eight people, like the room in the warehouse, but this one had bunk beds and giant murals of Bob Marley on the wall. There was no one else in the room, but six other bunks were tossed with messy linens and half-zipped backpacks. The room reeked of something stale and warm.

Jude and Bristol claimed the remaining two beds, a pair of side-by-side top bunks. The young man was still in the door.

"Buckingham Palace is pretty cool, and it's a good distance away from here so you can smoke while you walk. You can also just roll them up in our courtyard, we won't say anything and the neighbors are cool as long as you bring enough to share."

Jude sneered. "We don't—"

"We don't know if we'll make it out tonight. We're pretty beat. But we'll be here for a couple of weeks, so don't count us out."

The man smiled. "Cheers," he said, and closed the door behind him.

In spite of themselves, Bristol and Jude beamed at each other. They spoke at the same time.

"Showers!"

"Beds!"

They'd taken one bag for the two of them, which included a change of clothes for each of them, a few pairs of underwear and socks, toothbrushes, toothpaste, and soap. There was one shower in the warehouse for several dozen workers, but here there was a bathroom with two showers for every shared dormitory. Bristol pushed his anger and heartbreak down and let the respite of the water pressure rise to the forefront. Drying off afterward felt like being born again. He massaged the rented terry towel over his shoulders and felt the dead flakes give way to clean-feeling skin.

Jude was already asleep by the time Bristol had finished in the bathroom. He changed into clean underwear and slipped between the clean sheets. A few weeks of sleeping on the floor and washing in the sink had made him soft. He drank in the freshness of the sheets and the softness of the pillow, trying to soak the goodness of it all into his pores, trying to forget what Samara had been through. What they'd all been through.

Bristol was a creator, not a planner. Denver had told him to go back, marry Cindy, get citizenship. Then he'd be able to sponsor her as well as Jude, who'd they'd claim as a younger brother. After that, Denver and Jude would be able to take a flight to Canada and infiltrate the United States, contacting the Bird and getting his help to plant the same surveillance devices that Stephen was supposed to bring. He looked over at Jude and wondered if he was scared. Bristol was certainly scared. And the scariest thing he had to do was to marry his agent.

He wasn't sure it'd be possible. It was clear to see that Cindy had feelings for Bristol, but now more than ever, Bristol wanted nothing but to live with Samara by themselves in a little apartment or room or goddamn cardboard box. It didn't matter as long as people would just leave them alone.

The door to the room opened, and a couple of girls from somewhere in Asia, by the sound of their razor-cut language, came in noisily to try on some different outfits to go out in that evening. The party outside in the courtyard was just getting started with some bass and beats and low laughter. Bristol rolled onto his side. Two positive elements he would miss about the warehouse was silence at night and distance from fools. But then, if his birth hadn't gone the way it did—say he was born in another country, to an alternate family—would his life be so different from theirs? Would he have the same urge to create, the same affinity for solitude, or would he convince himself that he didn't have the time for it while traveling and getting drunk with friends or stoned with new acquaintances?

He would never be glad to have seen the horrors he'd seen, but he was, in a twisted way, grateful. He knew how precious time could be. He'd be damned if he'd waste it away.

The girls shrieked when someone else—another friend, by the sounds of it—walked into the room and turned on the lights. With that, he threw off the sheet. The girls stopped chatting and gave him an up-and-down appraising glance. He turned from them and pulled on his pants.

They giggled. "Nice legs," one of them said.

Bristol turned out the lights. "My friend needs to sleep."

"Oh, sorry, we didn't know he was up there." She grabbed a handful of her own hair and shook it out over the crown of her head. "I'm Lilly. What are you doing tonight? Want to go out with us?"

Bristol looked at her and, as he always did when he saw beautiful women, thought of Samara. What if her birth had also been different? He saw the young adulthood Samara deserved better than he saw an alteration of his own. She'd spend her Saturday nights dancing instead of freezing and watching for enemies in an abandoned monastery. She'd talk with girlfriends about shoes instead of legislation. She'd go on dates instead of...

"No thank you." Bristol's voice had softened in seconds, but Lilly didn't even seem to notice. She struck a flirtatious pose, and Bristol could almost see her watching only herself in her mind's eye. "You girls have fun. Don't forget about my friend, please. He needs to rest."

"We get it," said Lilly. "We've been at the pub all day too. Then sightseeing. So much walking. Had a long day, did he?" Lilly asked.

"Yes, he did," said Bristol, and the girls giggled again. Bristol reached for the doorknob. *May you never be asked to rise to half of his challenges.* "Yes. He did."

Bristol swiped a piece of yellow sidewalk chalk—one of the many toys lingering around for these overgrown children—from the lobby and walked until he saw a posh-looking community with little coffee houses, yogurt shops, and dress boutiques. Behind a shop that sold "artisan gifts," he drew Samara's face on the door to the back entrance. He was getting better at her eyes. He made them relaxed, not girlish and wide, but true to how she normally looked at him—with familiarity and ongoing exhaustion. He made her lips full, with highlights to show their exquisite thickness. When he was finished, the image of her face looked back at him with one finger drawn to her lips. He hoped it would communicate what he needed it to: *Shhhh.*

CHAPTER TWENTY-TWO

"WHEN IS THIS TRUCK SCHEDULED TO DEPART?" DENVER ASKED.

Taye consulted his tablet, tapping his fingers on the screen several times before answering. "Tomorrow morning."

Denver smiled. Her mother used to say that there was no greater contentment than working on something you were suited for. Back then, she and Bristol would glance at each other with gritted teeth, wondering if she knew about Bristol's nightly escapades and controversial murals. Now, she remembered her mother's words and felt the truth of them in her bones. "The customers will be happy to be getting their packages early. Tell the driver he's ready to go."

Denver and Taye ran through the checklist once more to see that everything was accounted for on the truck and then shut the door. Denver rapped the back of it twice, and the driver took off. The sun hadn't even set, but they were done for the day.

"Should we have a meeting tonight, then?" asked Taye.

"I could use a few hours to get things ready for tomorrow..."

"I'll set the alarm early so we can prep in the morning. We need to hear the others' ideas about getting you and Jude back to the US."

"I'm not sure if Samara's ready."

Taye raised an eyebrow. Denver could guess what he was thinking, that it was she that wasn't ready. And that was true. Samara simply hadn't healed, but how could she when she was stuck here? Her wounds were too raw. She'd feel better once she was in a new place, doing things she enjoyed. Deep down, Denver was afraid that if they did get back to Scotland, then back to America, then she'd be flooded with memories of Stephen and their life together. The two of them in Bristol's apartment, reading at opposite ends of the couch with their feet resting in the other's lap, too tired to talk but still intent on remaining connected. The two of them on the airship, holding onto each other as if trying to convince the other one that things would work out. The two of them in America, relishing in the surprises they were learning about each other. How could she face those places with him gone?

She also realized she didn't have much of a choice. If options were what she wanted, she'd have to work for them. "Okay. Tell the others to meet in the office in an hour."

"The office where Samara was assaulted? No. It's a nice day. Let's meet outside by the dumpsters."

"Good point. But we can't let anyone hear us. Let's meet in our room."

Taye groaned but turned to go inside and spread the news. Denver went straight to where she knew Samara would be after a hard day of work.

Samara had taken to hiding in a bathroom stall in the stretches of time between work and sleep. Sure enough, her feet were visible under the door in flat brown shoes with one broken lace and both soles peeling backward. Denver made a mental note to buy her a new pair if she had any money left after their train tickets.

"Hey," said Denver, trying to keep her voice soft. She waited a long time for an answer.

"Hey."

Denver cleared her throat. She was hopeless at this kind of thing. She tried channeling her mother, her softness and her warmth. "If you're feeling up to it, we're going to meet in an hour. We're getting out of here."

Again, there was a long pause before Samara answered. "Did you hear from Bristol?"

"Not yet."

"Do you think he's...gotten his green card already?"

"I don't know. Have you eaten?"

"No."

Denver sighed. So much for being maternal.

Samara sniffed. "I don't know how to do this. I don't know how to go on. How did you do it? After the baby. After Stephen. How were you able to just pick up and move on?"

"I wasn't. I didn't. Everything that happened is still a part of me, and it always will be. You'll always carry your experience with you, but it doesn't mean you have to stop living. When I think about Stephen, it makes me sad, but the thought of him also energizes me in a way, like I have to get moving or else his mission will die too. What that monster did to you, he did because he saw you as a victim to be used, not a survivor about to make history. What message does it send if you stay holed up in the bathroom?"

Samara was so quiet. Denver knocked on her door. "Samara! It doesn't have to be meaningless. We can give it meaning!"

Samara walked out of the stall—a good sign—and went to the sink to splash water on her face. With the tips of her fingers, she made large circles around her eyes.

"I was never very talented at this kind of thing. I faked it. But the truth was that I never knew what I was doing, and that was when I was...whole. I'm sure I'll just be a burden now."

"Carrying burdens makes you stronger. We need you there."

Samara stood straight and looked into the mirror. "I haven't really looked at myself since it happened." She dug her fingers into her scalp and teased her hair.

Denver winced. "Maybe I can do your hair before the meeting."

"Maybe we can do each other's. I do like it wild like this, though."

Denver nodded. "We'll keep the wildness and just cut off the ends. For you."

"You want one too? I have to warn you, I'm no good at hair."

Denver's was bound back in a tight bun. It kept it out of her face, but she didn't like the headache she'd learned to expect by midday. There was only one solution, and the prospect was looking better and better. "You don't need to be good for what I have in mind."

Samara went into the little room before Denver. Denver had cut off the ends, yes, but she kept the mass of curls around Samara's face, letting Samara hide behind them. When Denver walked in after her, the boys gasped.

"What did you do?" asked Taye.

Denver tried to mimic her mothers' stern face as she looked at Taye. She set a notebook down on the edge of the sink in their room. "I got some notes together about some recent news stories about the United States. What did you do?"

"You...shaved your head!"

"Wrong. Samara shaved my head."

Samara surveyed her from the side, just above her left ear. "I think I did a pretty good job, too."

"It...I mean I guess it's fine while we're here. Won't you want hair when you're back in Scotland, though?"

"No fuss. No literal or figurative headaches. Why would I want hair when it comes with all those things?"

"I just..." Taye glanced at his brothers. Cork stared, and Henry turned on his heel and dug in his little navy blue backpack.

"I'm not afraid of any boys not liking it, if that's what you're suggesting. In fact, I'm trying to minimize distractions, not add them."

Taye looked insulted. "I'm not!"

"Then what?" Samara asked.

"It's...it's..." Taye seemed to know what he wanted to say, but was searching for the right words for his thought. "Cold as balls in Edinburgh! Even in the spring and summer!"

Little Henry had found what he'd been looking for—a thick knit hat. "Nurse Sue made it for me," he said.

Denver felt the joints in her fingers soften as she took the hat from Henry. She thought about how she used to live her life, so very trusting. How did she find herself in this pattern of not trusting anyone else?

"Thank you, Henry."

Instead of putting it on, Denver held the hat to her heart. It was good to be so close to Nurse Sue. She remembered the times she'd seen Nurse Sue make these little things for the younger kids, sitting in the chair in the corner of the common room in Olympic Village when everyone else was loafing around watching the news. The nurse had lovingly threaded the yarn between her fingers, wrapping it around her needle in a meditative motion. Denver had even been vaguely jealous of the recipients. Back when she was pregnant for those few precious weeks, everyone fussed over her, the expectant mother. When she was no longer that, she went back to the role she'd had before. Hardened. Stoic. A leader without emotional needs. For the first time since Stephen died, this little gift, given in love, made in love, stirred something inside her. Her throat tightened.

Cork shook his head at Denver in a manner that strongly reminded her of Jude. "You're going to be so cold."

Denver laughed a bit and wiped away the beginnings of a tear. "If all goes according to plan, I'm about to go on an unsupported spy mission to a hostile country. I can handle a little cold."

CHAPTER TWENTY-THREE

IN THEIR NEW APARTMENT IN LONDON, JUDE WASHED BRISTOL'S brushes at the sink. Though it was technically the kitchen sink, it was dotted with the colorful hues that they'd made in their short stay here. Jude cleaned it with harsh chemicals every night to keep it looking nice—this wasn't his place, and he was determined to keep it clean. If they had anything less than an exemplary idea of how refugees lived, he'd prove them wrong.

Jude wasn't surprised when a wealthy art collector had recognized Bristol's chalk portrait of Samara and lurked around Camden Town until he eventually ran into him. He wasn't surprised when the wealthy man, proud to be an underground patron of one of the most elusive artists in recent memory, gave them use of one of his apartments to live and make art in. He wasn't even surprised that, once his dealer got involved, Bristol's paintings started selling for thousands of pounds in less than a full week in the city. What finally surprised him, in the end, was the alleged identity of the highest bidder.

"Tom Armistead." The dealer, whose name was Albert, wiped beads of sweat from his upper lip with a checkered cloth kerchief.

Jude didn't even bother turning the water off. He massaged the paint from the bristles. "Tom?"

Albert reached over and turned the faucet until the water stopped. "Armistead."

The name did sound familiar, but he assumed that this was yet another well-known aspect of the art world that everyone else knew except for him. "Does Bristol know?"

"Not yet, no. You're aware then? Of his ties?"

"Bristol probably would be."

"We mustn't bother Mr. Ray about this. He needs space. To create."

Since coming here, everyone had always treated Bristol as something he wasn't at all: purely a creator, living in isolation from the rest of humanity. Every native seemed to shield him from any news from their home country, or any unfairness in the entire world, whether or not the United States was involved. But what, Jude wondered, would he paint if he wasn't an advocate first?

Jude put the clean brushes back in the tin coffee can. "Tell me about Tom Armistead."

"Armistead is the grandson of a very famous American. In fact, his father is a government employee, and he is rumored to do occasional government work himself."

"Either he's employed in a Metrics agency or he isn't. There are no contractors in the United States. People there get one job all of their lives."

Albert smirked, the lithe lines of his body relaxing. "Things may have changed."

"Things don't change there."

"If they didn't, wouldn't you still be there?"

Jude tapped the paintbrushes on the edge of the sink, hoping to get a few spatters on Albert's elegant casual clothes. He hated when people tried so hard to make you think they weren't trying hard. "Does it matter? About Armistead?"

"Well, yes, actually it does." Albert glanced over his pressed sweatshirt. There were the miniature manufactured tears, but no water or paint spots. Oh, well. Maybe next time.

"It does," Albert continued. "In fact, most people would say it matters quite a bit that a malicious dictatorship is buying artwork that criticizes its own policies, wouldn't you?"

Jude froze. He scoured his memory again for the name Armistead, but no revelations came. "If that's what happening, yes, it does matter." Jude placed the brushes back in the can and dried his hands with a frayed tea towel. "If that's what's happening."

"I don't believe letting him know would be in Mr. Ray's best interest. Promise you'll not say a word."

The floorboards creeped subtly to alert Jude that Bristol was right outside the doorway. "Okay," he said. "I promise I won't tell him."

"Won't tell me what?" Bristol asked, stepping into the kitchen.

"That the United States Government is buying your pieces. For large sums of money. For reasons unknown," Jude said, exaggerating his doe-eyed innocence.

Albert shot a quick scowl at Jude and turned to Bristol. "It's nothing we can't handle. We can ban him from the auction, refuse to do business with him."

"With who? I thought Jude said it was Metrics."

"It's a person associated with Metrics. A Tom Armistead." Albert fished out a business card to make sure he had the name correct, then held it out to Bristol, who squinted at it. Albert quickly pocketed the card.

"Shall I contact him?"

Instead of answering Albert, Bristol addressed Jude. "John Armistead saved me right at the start of the relocation. I would have frozen to death in a walk-in freezer if it hadn't been for him."

"Do you think there's any connection?"

"There aren't that many last names anymore, since people started having just one child to carry the names on. It could be a coincidence, but I have to believe they at least know each other."

Jude nodded, and Albert looked impatient. "I'll contact him for you then, Mr. Ray. Ask him to please thank his dear cousin for his help—"

"If you could just give me his contact information, Jude and I will take it from there."

"I'm so sorry, Mr. Ray, but I keep my clients' information quite confidential."

"But he's the artist," said Jude. "Surely he'd be glad to hear from him if he's buying his paintings."

Albert crossed his thin arms, interlacing one behind the other in a snakelike movement. "I do try not to make exceptions."

"Fine." Bristol crossed the room and opened the door. "You're fired."

Albert gaped momentarily, but quickly regained his composure. "Mr. Ray, that would be unwise. Your benefactor hired me to sell the art you create in his apartment. I suggest you discuss my policies and my employment with him."

"Oh, we can leave right now," said Jude, almost chirping. "You don't have to scare us with poverty. Bristol and I have been in worse spots."

"Ever slept in a tree, Al? We have." Bristol clapped Jude vigorously on the shoulder. Jude squeezed his stomach muscles in so he wouldn't fall forward. "Ever run from people who want you deported? Or dead? Ever have only one thing to lose? We're not afraid of starting over. We've got more important fish to fry, if you know what I mean."

"Give us the card. It'll be easier on you."

Albert reached inside his pocket and fingered the card. "Just because you've struggled doesn't mean I haven't. I've spent quite a bit of time on my business—"

"Oh, for god's sake, give me that." Bristol reached for Albert's pants pocket. Instead of protecting the card, Albert swooped his shoulders back and thrust his hips toward Bristol's hands.

"Artists," said Albert breathlessly. "I suppose this kind of passion is the reason I got into this business in the first place.

Jude turned away in disgust, not at the flirtatious comment, but at the willingness to give his fight up so easily. It truly was a wonder how the human species had survived since most of them weren't nearly stubborn enough.

If Bristol was embarrassed, he didn't show it. He simply tucked the card inside his black hoodie and said, "Thank you, Albert. I promise I won't reach out to him until my sister gets here."

"Oh?" said Albert, still clearly overwhelmed. "I didn't realize you were expecting company."

"Any day now. My sister and a few friends. Jude called them with the address this morning."

"Where will they stay?"

"This is a big place."

"Three bedrooms. Only one bathroom. Not ideal for guests. Maybe they should stay at the hostel you found when you arrived?"

"Don't worry, Bristol can paint with them around," Jude said. "Our friends won't affect your income."

"Famous last words," said Albert. He looked distinctly annoyed that Jude was still in the room. "Well, I'll pop by again tomorrow to check in, Mr. Ray. You're sure you don't want me to ask Armistead about the nature of his purchases?"

"No, thank you. We'll handle it from here."

"Cheers."

Albert slinked past Bristol to grab his messenger bag and leave. Once he was gone, they both examined the card. It said:

TOM ARMISTEAD
WATCH ID: 22591049

"He's a Two," Bristol noted, tapping the first digit of the ID. "So was John. Most Twos do work for Metrics."

"Yeah, my parents did." Jude left out the part that he'd always assumed he would too, though he'd been afraid, terribly afraid, that his job assignment would have a title that implied low responsibility. Research associate, maybe, or operations coordinator. "Do you think Metrics is really buying your paintings?"

"I have an inkling they are."

"Why would they do that?"

"Because they're trying to convince the world that they're not as bad as we know they are. They want people, especially people in the UK, to think that they're open minded enough to take us back. Did you see the news today?"

Jude nodded. The United States had hinted that they were willing to give up their nuclear program in exchange for security guarantees. And, of course, their escaped citizens back, so they could be brought to "justice."

"I do have a few questions I want to ask him," said Bristol, fingering the card, "but I need to talk to the girls."

Jude nodded. The last part was obvious. Things tended to go very badly when they didn't include the girls.

CHAPTER TWENTY-FOUR

SAMARA WAS DROPPING OFF HER LAST PACKAGE WHEN JUDE AND Bristol arrived. She'd gone back to working and was surprised at how much she liked it now. Before, not having access to information that could help them or anyone to talk with had been a burden. Now it was a benefit. She only concerned herself with the numbers on her little pager. Walk, walk, pick up, walk, walk, dump. Repeat. With the efficiencies that Denver had put into place, they were working eight-hour shifts instead of fourteen, but Samara could have done much more.

She squinted at her beeper, though Denver had coded an algorithm into the system that prevented the floor staff from receiving orders past five, and it was 5:01. The end of the work day meant sifting through the news with Denver and taking notes on anything relevant, which would have been more than welcome a few weeks ago. Now she hoped for another set of numbers to pop up to give her a small task to do and grab that instant, though minuscule, sense of completion.

She hung her apron and deposited her pager in the paint-chipped box hanging on the wall and went upstairs to do her nightly news shift. The younger boys, Cork and Henry, would do something useful while Taye made his rounds to the other warehouses in the area to make friends with whoever could obtain fake citizenship documents for them. She wanted to ask him if he'd had any luck yet, but she also never wanted to talk with any man ever again, so she figured that he'd tell her if he'd made any progress. He almost never spoke to her anymore, but today he made a beeline for her. She instinctively braced herself.

"It's okay," he said, raising both hands. "I have good news. One, Denver and Jude both have fake passports now."

So they would travel back to the most dangerous country in the world as soon as they could get on a flight. Yeah. Great news. Still, it was a block heaved out of the way. She wanted to congratulate him, though she'd never doubted his smooth nature. Taye always got what he wanted.

"Two, Bristol and Jude just pulled in. They're taking us back to London with them tonight."

Samara raised her head and looked around. Bristol and Denver were locked in a hug with Jude standing by. As she looked, Taye smirked.

She looked at him. "What?"

"That's the first time I've seen you smile since...you know. The first time in a while."

She hadn't even noticed, but now that he'd mentioned it, her face did feel uncommonly light. "I'm glad they're back. It'll be good to get back to London and get on with what's really important."

"What's really important, Samara?"

In her old life, Samara would have rolled her eyes at that, maybe jabbed at him a little. But she didn't have time or interest for these games anymore. "What's really important is getting our information back from America. Getting Denver and Jude over there, then back again as quick as possible."

"That's important, yeah. But I know what matters most to you."

"Why do you always make this about you?"

"That's what I'm saying!" Taye reached for the top of his head and staggered back. "It's not about me at all! I thought maybe if I came back with, you know, a little more money and a little more experience with women, you'd forget about him and we could find a way to make us work. But you two are too deep in each other's' lives. It's like each of you live inside the other's head."

Samara's heart quickened its pace as it always did when someone said something true but utterly inconvenient. What was more inconvenient was drawing closer to someone at a time like this.

"At this point, Samara, I just want you to be happy. I know you don't feel like it right now, but you're special."

"I am not special. I don't even want to be special."

"Well, don't worry, you're not, like, 'the chosen one' or anything." He laughed a laugh she'd heard so many times before when he was joking around with new friends and acquaintances. Maybe that's what they were now. "I just mean you have some gifts, and it's nice to see you use them to help other people. You can encourage. You can nurture. You can lead. You have a teacher's heart, and you need to draw energy from whoever is going to bring out the best in it."

"I was never any good at taking compliments."

"You're welcome. My point is that if you think you can't be together because of everything that's happening, you're wrong. That's exactly why you should be together. We're stronger that way. We've spent our whole lives being told what to do, who to do it with, and when. Now, we get to make our own decisions. And the best decisions are the ones that help you grow."

"Very inspirational."

"You're welcome again. And you know, now that I successfully secured passports for Jude and Denver, Bristol doesn't have to go back to Scotland at all," Taye said. "For anything," he added with far more dramatic emphasis than necessary.

"You don't have to spell everything out for me, but thanks."

"You've been spending too much time around Denver."

"What do you have against Denver?"

"Nothing at all. Leaders should be forward. But you used to be nicer."

"Nah, you're just lucky I liked you."

"Supremely. But you never loved me like you loved Bristol. I can wait for someone who thinks of me like you think of him. And you're lucky, too, since you don't have to."

"That's exactly Bristol's argument, you know. That we should be together because we can."

"Smart guy."

"There just...always seemed to be better things to do."

"Than love?"

Samara's mind flashed to her parents. They'd been in love. Not quite how she was in love with Bristol, although it may have been that way at one time. They'd met for the first time on their wedding day, like every married couple under Metrics, and somehow got from that to the kind of love where they looked out for each other, needed each other to stay afloat. Her dad had started drinking, illegally, when Metrics took her mom away. And although she thought of them every day, she didn't really worry. They were together; they had to be. It made sense. They would have found each other again. It racked her with guilt to know that they thought she'd been killed, but knowing they must be together comforted her. They would be devastated together, and the way they were together, that devastation would have been worlds healthier than if they'd been left to deal with that news on their own. Their love was a love of usefulness and ease. She'd grown up with this kind of love in her home, and yet she wasn't able to recognize and harness it when it came for her. Now that she stopped and thought about it, the question seemed ridiculous. Better things to do than love? She'd been working at half-strength.

"Come on," said Taye, breaking her trance. "Let's go see them."

In the office, Bristol loomed, the muscles in his neck prominently catching the light.

Her hair had been cut, but random curls still sprang from her ponytail. Her body had always been curvy, but her jumpsuit still hung limply from it. There was nothing about her appearance that made her feel good other than seeing Bristol's face and knowing he was glad to see her. More than glad. Seeing herself that way, through cherishing eyes, warmed her. She took him in too. He was the same height as ever, slightly taller than her, but only noticeable if they were close. But something about him seemed different. He seemed larger in an invisible sense. Just standing there, he seemed more sure of himself. More stable. Rooted in something, though Samara couldn't tell what it was.

"Samara got a haircut while you were away too," said Denver, breaking the silence.

"Didn't go for drama like you, though, huh?" he said to his sister.

"I've had enough of it." Samara couldn't stop staring at him. Of course Taye was right. Of course she was in love with him. But admitting it to herself couldn't be the only thing that was different. Slowly, it dawned on her what she must have been seeing. The way he was standing, the easy way he held his jaw...it was just how she felt when she knew something. "Bristol?"

He grinned. "Samara?"

"What happened?"

When Bristol clicked his tongue, Samara's suspicions were confirmed. He did know something after all.

"So much," he said and dragged some chairs into a circle. Jude and Denver sat. "So, so much."

CHAPTER TWENTY-FIVE

BRISTOL TOLD THEM ABOUT EVERYTHING. THE CHALK PORTRAIT of Samara. The wealthy benefactor. The bidder who may have been acting on behalf of Metrics. They agreed it made sense.

"What does this mean for our mission?" asked Denver.

"I think you and Jude should still go, and plant the surveillance devices. We need to reveal their plan so we can put a wet blanket on the idea that they're suddenly open-minded and ready to join the world community with no consequences," said Samara.

Bristol's heart skipped. After all these years, Jude was every bit as close to Samara as Denver was to him. He didn't want to see Denver go, and he was sure Samara didn't want to see Jude go either, but if they were smart—and they were—the potential to reach so many other lives was too great to pass up. This was their chance to save their parents, their friends, and everyone else Metrics would ever wrong. There was no option B. They could not just avoid trouble. More trouble would come to them. He knew Samara understood this and he longed to talk to her about it, but here they were, in yet another room planning strategy. He reminded himself, as he had to often, that she'd rejected him more than once. He tried to focus on the task at hand, but all he could focus on was the last time they were together in his bed and how the light had spread across her bare skin like a sunrise.

"I don't know. What do you think, Bristol?" Jude asked.

All eyes turned to him.

Samara's clouded face began to break a smile. "Will you test our theory?" He said nothing, so she elaborated. "That Metrics is buying your art to prop up its own position in the world? Will you paint a collage of what's coming and see if they buy it?"

They wanted him to paint a collage of the genocide of the Fives? Samara's parents were Fives. Had she suggested this?

"I...I'll try."

"We are beyond 'try,' little brother," said Denver with her signature eye roll. "Do it. Make it gruesome and realistic."

"Hopefully, it'll provide a visual, emotional reaction to the evidence we collect," said Samara. "And if they don't bid on it like they've bid on the other stuff, it'll look terrible politically. We'll finally be able to convince the United Countries to install a new government and grant amnesty to refugees."

"No problem. I'll start it as soon as we can get back to London. We'll have to take two trips. The car that Albert loaned to me can only take four at a time."

"We won't need two trips. Taye and his brothers are going to stay here and run the warehouse," said Samara.

"Seriously?" asked Jude. "After all that's happened here?"

"That's exactly why he wants to do it. Otherwise, the owner will just put some cheap manager in place. I wanted him to stay and protect the people here."

Denver ran a hand over the crown of her head. "I asked him not to, but he insists. For the sake of all of us here and in hiding elsewhere, we really need to go and come back. I've adjusted the identities that the UK originally made for Stephen and Jude. The ID numbers are different, and the retinal patterns, but I couldn't adjust the blood type or fingerprints."

"I could," said Jude. "The only thing we'll need to do is sync them with the passports that Taye got for us. Birthdays, coordinates of origin, that kind of stuff."

"Did it right before you walked in, slick." Denver said.

Samara put her hands on her hips. "You two are going to be unstoppable."

"If you think you'll need me, I can still go find Cindy. I think she'd understand," said Bristol.

Denver scoffed. "You had a watch for what—a month? You can't code, you can't hack, you wouldn't know a network from a nanometer."

"Hey—"

"Probably true," said Jude. "Do you even know the difference between a server and a servo?"

"Or a database from a driver?" asked Samara.

"Or a DNS from a DRAM?"

"Okay! Okay! I get the point." Bristol crossed his arms high on his chest. "I have other gifts."

"Yes, you do. You need to use them where they're most useful. Make that tableau just awful."

"Denver's right," said Samara. "The outside world has already decided that your work has monetary value. Now, it needs to have political value too. Go for controversy here, and when they get back, we'll release it just as we're releasing the proof that Metrics is about to kill the Fives. We'll appeal to both reason and emotion. That's what our problem has been before—we tried appealing to both, but neither was strong enough."

"Although you'd really think it would be. People here knew about the mass murder of the Unregistered. They knew that the reason we were here was because we wanted to hang onto our lives, not because we wanted to take their jobs," said Bristol.

"But it wasn't powerful enough. They didn't have visual evidence or audio recordings. The only evidence the public was told about was experts agreeing that according to fly over missions, there appeared to be proof that Metrics had murdered its people. From a public relations standpoint, that couldn't be weaker. And then we showed up wanting work, but to them, the two seemed unrelated. They didn't make an emotional connection, they just had to trust the experts."

"And see us as human beings," said Bristol.

"Which they couldn't do because they couldn't see themselves in our spot. But this is our chance." This was the most Samara had said in weeks. She felt the strain in her voice and knew the others could hear it. "Get over there, collect some proof, and get back. If this works, we can finally...we can finally be..."

Breathless, she found she could not say it. It was a dream that she'd held for so long, and it was so close now that she could feel it in the lump in her throat, the tremble in her hands, and the ache between her shoulders. It seemed so important, now more than ever, for her own safety and dignity, and for the future she hoped to have with Bristol.

Jude was the one to help her. "Free."

CHAPTER TWENTY-SIX

DENVER BUCKLED HER SEATBELT AS SOON AS THEY BOARDED SO the airship host could walk by without reminding her. She was about to snap at Jude to do the same, but he was just tightening the last remaining shoulder strap. She huffed and fiddled with her watch, adjusting the time to Eastern Standard. One glance over at Jude's wrist and she saw that he'd done that too.

She couldn't stop having these moments of desire to rub his nose in the fact that he'd utterly destroyed the last mission. She knew that's not what Stephen would have done, but because of this little ass, Stephen wasn't here. But Jude kept surprising her.

"Good morning, folks, and welcome aboard Air Canada. This flight is scheduled to arrive in Toronto in just about two hours and thirty-three minutes. Please stay seated with your straps securely fastened at each of the five points...two shoulders, two hips, and one—whoops, my co-captain tells me I'm not allowed to say that word."

The other passengers chuckled politely, but Denver sighed. The last buckle connected the other straps at the crotch.

"Just sit back and enjoy the flight, folks."

All around her on the circular floor, people settled in, turning their eyes to their watches or printed reading material. Jude pulled out a paperback and opened it to the middle. Denver fumed. Of course he was the type to dog-ear his pages.

"What are you doing? Where did you get that?"

He lowered it. "It was just lying around the apartment in London. The guy who lived there before us left an awful lot of romances on the shelf."

"We should be prepping." Denver snatched the book from his hands and immediately regretted it. Several passengers facing her direction looked up.

Jude just folded his hands. "Okay, but I don't think we should go into much detail. I know most of the world isn't as paranoid as the United States, but there could still be people or machines listening."

"Let's just practice." She tapped the face of her watch and waited until he did the same. "How are you enjoying your flight so far?"

"Much better than the first time I flew." The pace of his words was calm but purposeful.

"Oh? I deeply appreciated that ride. What a shame you're not more grateful."

"I didn't say I wasn't grateful. I'm just glad the lights are working on this ship."

The passenger on the other side of Jude spoke up, though he was also on his watch. "No lights on the last flight? It wasn't this airline, was it?"

"No, sir, it wasn't."

The first time had been in a British military airship. The officers had given them space blankets, but had then shuffled them into the dark airship with closed windows so there was no sunlight for the blankets to absorb. There were no seats and definitely no seatbelts—it was a cargo ship. Now that she was years removed from that experience, it made sense that they would use one to pick up the refugees, since cargo ships traveled back and forth to Canada all the time and they were just south of the border. They'd shivered in the dark for hours, but they had been together—all of them—and the ship had taken them to another country, which may just as well have been another world for them. Before then, they'd had no idea that there were other countries. Metrics convinced its people, from birth, that they were a worldwide government, so they thought the imaginary lines dividing countries had long been dissolved, just as the lines between states had been under Metrics. Denver remembered seeing the brilliant shades of green for the first time and how the beauty of the hills next to the sea took her breath away. Scotland, from the sky, was the most stunning sight she'd ever seen. When they saw it, Denver and Stephen had been locked arm-in-arm, determined never to be separated again. When the windows had opened and they were hit with those impossible colors, it felt as if a new world had been opened to them, one with opportunity and a future that just went on and on.

As Jude made friendly conversation with his seatmate with both eyes still glued to his watch, Denver slouched into her seat as much as her straps would allow. The one perk about going on this mission with this stupid kid was that she didn't care much whether or not she ever came back.

They landed in Toronto and checked into a hotel that was so old that it was still advertising the fact that they offered holoTV in all rooms. They'd traveled light, just a couple of changes of clothes each, one pair of shoes, which they wore, and holowatches with encrypted files that held codes. They only needed to hack into the Internet in one location and upload those codes into the watches of three targets to listen and read conversations that would prove that Metrics was planning to murder entire generations of men, women, and children in a class that had recently become economically useless.

CHAPTER TWENTY-SEVEN

BRISTOL NOTED THE CHARCOAL COATING THE TIPS OF HIS fingers and scratched his nose by rubbing it on his wrist instead. He knew that he could have used any medium to produce the scene of the murder of the Fives, but he figured the art sector would be more interested—and thereby give him more press, and thereby reach more people—if he paid attention to his materials. He considered lots of things, but needed something quick enough to have a final product as soon as Denver and Jude returned. Money didn't really seem to matter, because as soon as his benefactor heard what he was planning, he was beside himself to offer any assistance he needed to get the project going. In the end, he unthreaded some of the clothing they'd arrived here in, had it re-woven into a largish multi-textural piece of cloth, bleached it, and then stretched it onto a canvas. Instead of using common willow or vine charcoal, he decided to take a crack at making his own. He wanted to char some small branches from American Eastern White Pines—his benefactor was more than happy to arrange this—and mix those with the ashes of dead animals from the local veterinary clinic nearby. The benefactor, an animal lover, had frowned upon this, but had looked the other way when Bristol approached the clinic. The clinic director had shrugged and handed Bristol a small box containing ashes. Before sending them away to be burned together and made into charcoal, Bristol had gathered his courage. He wasn't thinking big enough. He approached several funeral homes instead without telling his benefactor. The first funeral director was stunned and asked Bristol if he'd considered the "ethical implications" of using human remains in his work. He said he had. He wouldn't be here if what he was about to take on was anything of marginal importance. One by one, crematorium directors slammed doors in his face until finally, he spoke with one who said that under absolutely no circumstances would he donate ashes to his cause—but if he were to come back on a Friday, he may run into a junior mortician who would be cleaning the equipment. When he did, the junior associate gave him a small red plastic bag. "These are all mixed together," he explained. "It's nobody in particular. It's really just residue." Bristol assured him, as respectfully as he could muster, that this was perfect.

The pencils were ready within a few days. Drawing on the canvas made of their clothing with the pencils made of dead trees and humans changed the experience for Bristol into something completely new. Suddenly he wasn't just focused on the outcome of the image, but showing respect to the materials. He was careful not to waste, so he had to hold the pencils gently so they wouldn't break. He wouldn't make a habit of using these materials, but he hoped his muscle memory would take over the next time he drew. He liked this kind of drawing, even though it wasn't completely natural for him. More delicate, more reverent.

He'd been in his studio for a few days before he realized that even though he and Samara were now alone in the apartment, he hadn't fantasized about her once. He was proud of himself for finally getting over her before he remembered again that she'd had a traumatizing experience and he hadn't thought to check in with her. Even if he finally was free of her gravitational pull, he didn't want to lose her as a friend. He kept searching for a good time, but she left the apartment for long stretches of time and wouldn't come back until late, when all Bristol wanted to do was sleep. It was a shame, because he desperately needed some company apart from Albert. He'd come over every few days to take pictures of the raw materials or emerging canvas or, most obnoxiously, Bristol himself.

"Where do your friends go all day? I haven't seen the little one in a while." Albert pointed a laser coming from his watch at Bristol's forehead.

"You said you wanted to take pictures of my pencils, not me," said Bristol.

"My clients want to see who commissioned the creation of these pencils. That's important too. Anyway, back to the question at hand. Where is Jude? Where are your guests?"

"This city is the center of the universe. The world capital of culture. I don't know, maybe they're at the museum. Maybe they're eating the best curry they've ever had. Maybe they're out listening to buskers at the park."

Albert's smile spread as he gazed down at his fingernails. "Maybe they're at the library picking apart the constitution with a fine-tooth comb."

"What?"

"A friend of mine works at the London Library. He says he's seen her there every day for nearly a week now, from open to close, working her way through the entire civics section and taking notes by hand. An aspiring lawyer, perhaps?"

"She's an ambitious woman."

"Well, it's none of my business really," said Albert, feigning nonchalance. One of the few things Bristol knew about him was how terrible he was at lying. He'd be hopeless at secret keeping. "I just thought that if you had a plan and wanted to share it with me, I could mention it to one of our clients. I'm sure they'd be interested in knowing the exact pressures under which this piece was created."

Bristol took a deep breath in, then sighed out loudly. "The others say I'm not allowed to tell you."

"Come now," said Albert. "We're old friends now, though, aren't we? And if this information can help me sell this—" he waved at the canvas, still obviously clueless about what he was looking at, "this—is it going to be oil on canvas?"

"It's just a charcoal."

"Oh." He looked disappointed. "Well, then it needs help all the more then. Tell me what you have planned. Are you planning to introduce new legislation in Britain? They tell me that's what you tried to do in Scotland. Or a new campaign to lobby the UC?"

Bristol rubbed his forehead and felt the grooves in his skin. "There's something coming, yes. I can't tell you what it is, but we hope that it will allow us to stay or go or do whatever we'd like. And hopefully that freedom would extend beyond us too."

"Do you mean all of the refugees? I've heard many are in hiding throughout Europe."

"All the people in the world."

"But most of us are not under their thumb."

"If you don't see us all as under their thumb, there's no way we can help each other." Bristol cast another eye at the drawing. It was unfair to ask cloth and coal to do this, to create empathy, and yet now it was more important than ever. "Tell your clients to guess, for all I care. They'll know soon enough."

"Oh, good, a guessing game," said Albert. "Just what everyone loves."

There was a loud knock at the door. It couldn't be Samara. It sounded like a police knock, but there was no voice afterward. Albert and Bristol looked at each other. Albert was clearly the more panicked of the two, so Bristol spoke calmly and slowly. "Tell them you're here to meet an artist and you don't know who. Say Mr. Kent asked you to come speak to the artist, but no one was here when you arrived." Albert nodded, and Bristol slipped into the hall closet, behind the heavy wall of coats.

Bristol heard Albert's light fingers turn the doorknob, but there was no police officer at the door. Instead, a deep voice rang in a Scottish accent. "I'm sorry, I think I must have the wrong door. I'm looking for my friends, Bristol Ray and Samara Shepherd."

Bristol bolted out of the closet, sending outerwear and shoes flying in all directions. "Daniel!"

Daniel smiled through his fuller-than-ever beard. "Had me going!"

They didn't have a hugging sort of relationship, but Bristol forgot that for a moment and opened his arms wide as if he was embracing a brother. Daniel stiffly patted his back, but Bristol couldn't have cared less—he was starving for a friendly face.

"Have they come for you yet?" asked Daniel. "Anyone?"

"Not yet. Have you heard from my sister?"

"We've heard from the Bird. They're at the capital, and they're together, but they haven't made contact with him yet."

"They're at the what?"

Bristol had completely forgotten that Albert was still in the room. He groaned, but Daniel turned and put his index finger directly in front of Albert's face. His arm, laced with tattoos up to his rolled-up short sleeve, bulged. "You'll keep our friends safe by keeping that to yerself, won't ya?"

"But they're at the capital? Of America? Now? Right under the nose of Metrics?"

"Daniel, this is Albert. He sells my work and works with the publicist. Albert, Daniel works for the Red Sea, the international aid group."

"In America, it was a rebel group," Albert muttered, as if reminding himself.

Daniel growled in his throat. "Before Metrics killed all the rebels, yeah."

"This is more than I was expecting," said Albert. "My clients will be very interested to know about this. I should say whatever happens next, the value of this piece will go up. This is now a piece of historical significance. There's no losing now." He was practically salivating. "But I do need to begin planting the seeds in the minds of buyers as soon as possible...most people don't make impulsive decisions about the kind of money this will bring us."

"No," said Bristol, locking eyes.

"Allow me to explain this. If the buyers don't realize that this is a piece of historical significance, we'll have to lower the price, and then that'll affect the price of your work—and perhaps even the future of your cause—for years to come. I won't tell everyone. Only serious buyers."

"You just told me that Metrics itself is a serious buyer. My main buyer."

"Well," said Albert, suddenly sheepish, "We don't know that for sure."

Daniel brought himself up to his full height, towering over both men but glowering over Albert. "Do you care at all about his sister and his friend coming back? Do you know his brother-in-law was killed on the first attempt of this mission? Is that what you meant by there's no losing now?"

Bristol stepped in. "Don't say anything, Albert. Not until they come back. You don't know what they mean to me. I'd rip this canvas up in a heartbeat if there was a chance Metrics found out my sister was there."

Albert threw up his hands. "Fine! I just thought...but of course you're right...I'll wait. But I must tell this story eventually, and I'll need all the facts."

So you can distort them, thought Bristol, but he nodded in affirmation. Nothing about his life was ever easy, but having faith in people was the most difficult piece of this entire puzzle.

CHAPTER TWENTY-EIGHT

JUDE SCANNED THE HOTEL BALLROOM AND ASSESSED THE RISKS, acknowledged the exits, and checked out the targets, all while getting a new high score in Dazzleball. The secret, he learned but was too afraid to admit out loud, wasn't a secret at all. In fact, it had been Denver's advice from the beginning: practice. When he stopped thinking about it and started just doing it by rote, again and again, he learned that not only was he able to play mind-numbing games quickly, it actually helped free up his concentration, like he was giving busy work to the slow, thoughts-into-words part of his brain so the quick, react-in-real-time part of his brain didn't have to deal with it. He acknowledged that this was a skill that didn't exactly come naturally, and was a terrible distraction until he got good at it, and wondered how many other people had thought of the idea and followed through enough to push through the difficulty of practicing it. He hoped not many. He assumed everyone.

Common courtesy dictated that all sounds were either turned off or the music only played in individuals' earchips. Jude wore an earchip for optics, but had turned off the sound, which was good because when he heard his first target's feet move from across the room, he followed.

It was a large event—a National Day dinner for all the interns who worked in the capital—and Jude fit right in. His target, a man in his late fifties, walked to the bathroom. His name was Devon Davidson, and he worked for the Office of Societal Efficiency—the office that made the blueprints for the mass murders when the Ones decided that there were too many people and not enough work to do. He wasn't truly a decision maker, although he probably thought he was. Their research indicated that he was an arrogant man who had written about the removal of the lower classes since he was a student. Jude followed. All he needed to do was to get close enough to his watch to air-slip the code over to his watch. He should be able to do that with a urinal between them.

While the thinking part of his brain was too busy shepherding brightly colored balls in a net to be afraid, Jude opened the bathroom door a few counts after the target had walked in, paused his game, and froze. Somehow, despite the largeness of the space, there were only three urinals along the bathroom wall.

He wanted to give the whole plan up, but then he would have lost an entire evening, and they needed to leave this country as soon as possible. He selected the file, activated air-slip, and took the middle urinal. He did not acknowledge the other two men, nor did they acknowledge him. Davidson was on his left, still shooting a steady stream into the porcelain bowl, while the man on his right finished up, zipped and tucked, then walked out of the bathroom without washing his hands.

For a moment, it seemed like it was going to go off without a hitch. The air-slip had worked, and though the code prevented Davidson's watch from displaying it, the data was now being downloaded onto it. It was good that Jude didn't have much in his bladder, because he needed to share proximity with Davidson just a few minutes more in order for the data to completely download. Mercifully, Davidson went to the sink to wash his hands, and Jude followed close behind, staying to his side so their watches would be close as possible.

Davidson caught his eye and nodded in a friendly manner to Jude in the mirror. Jude mimicked him. Then, a dull buzz whispered to them both and Davidson looked down. When he looked up again, his face was all fury.

"You son of a bitch!" Davidson stepped forward, tapping his wrist.

"What? Oh, I'm sorry," said Jude, eyeing his watch. "I had air-slip set up to share some family photos with a friend. It must have activated early."

He glowered. "You'd better hope that I see you and a couple of old slobs here," he said and raised his wrist to his face, deep in concentration.

Jude took his chance. With the heel of his hand, he thrust his robotic hand upward, breaking Davidson's nose. He heard it crack and cringed. Even with all the adrenaline pumping, he didn't like violence. At least he wasn't able to feel it. He darted behind Davidson, felt his pulse with his forearm bone, and squeezed. Davidson stopped fighting immediately, which surprised Jude, but then again, when would he have had a need to fight in his life? He was a Two, probably with a perfect citizenship score. Jude dragged his unconscious body into a stall and locked the door. Hopefully, he wouldn't remember this encounter, but just in case, Jude took his watch, changed his movement pattern to make it look like he'd never left the ballroom so as not to jar his memory. He deleted the precious software so it wouldn't be found.

"Call Denver," he whispered into his watch as he glided out the door. The dinner was starting, and all the interns were moving to the banquet hall.

She didn't even bother to say hello.

"What are you doing? We said no calls!"

"The mission has been compromised. Davidson had an alarm system on his watch."

"Shit. Where is he now?"

"Unconscious in a bathroom stall."

"Go wipe his watch so no one finds him."

"Already done. But I think I should get out of here."

"Are you kidding? There are two more targets in that room. They should be together. Get the recording software installed as fast as you can."

"They're going to wonder where Davidson is eventually! And I can't lock the bathroom door. Sooner or later someone's going to go in there."

"Go find a janitor's closet and put a 'bathroom closed' sign on the door. I'm switching the security camera footage to show an empty hallway now. Should hold for a few minutes. Go."

Why hadn't he thought of that? Walking as fast as he could without running, he found a utility closet with a stand-up sign that read "closed for cleaning." He placed it in front of the bathroom and joined the banquet. All of the other interns were already seated, and the speaker was already making remarks. Even if he could find a seat now, how would he get close enough to his next target? At least the technology allowed him into the room, thanks to Denver. There was an invitation code on his watch. Otherwise, the security guards at the front would have immediately thrown him out.

He saw the waiters moving around the room in their black pants and pressed white shirts. This had to be, what, a five-course meal? Switching places with a server would give him just the proximity he needed to air-slip the codes to both watches and get out of here before the soup was served. He couldn't abide any more fighting, though, and he knew that's what Denver would suggest in order to get one of these uniforms.

He followed the man who'd refilled the waters of the front table. Just before he disappeared into the kitchen, he spoke to him his lowest voice.

"They're going to kill the Fives like they did the Unregs."

The man, undoubtedly a Five himself, looked up with wide eyes. "Wh-what?"

"They're going to kill the Fives. I'm one who got out. It's hard to explain, but I'm here to stop them. I need your uniform."

"My uniform?"

Jude nodded. "Please."

The man looked around, and Jude could almost see a wish to trade places with anybody else. "What am I going to do?"

Jude took him to the now-closed bathroom and traded clothes with him. "You can wait here. I'll be back afterward to switch back. I promise."

The man, not much older than Jude, nodded. "My friends and I thought they'd killed the Unregs, but my parents still insist that they're out west. How do you know for sure?"

"It's a long story. The rest of the world wants to stop a repeat, though. I'm getting proof right now so we can get some help."

"The rest of the world?"

"It's a long story," Jude repeated. "I'll be back soon. Don't mind the man in the stall. I promise I'll come back."

He went out, finishing out a shudder that started in his inner ear and shook him all the way out to his shoulders. He wasted no time setting up the slip—now he only needed to get close enough. The speaker was still up at the podium, and the water glasses were all full. Another Five server looked at him quizzically, perhaps wondering who this newcomer was and wondering where his friend went, but Jude could not risk letting another person in on his plan. He avoided eye contact. Another man came out of the kitchen with a basket full of bread. Jude inched closer to him.

"I'll do that," he said.

"Wait till she's done," said the server, indicating the woman speaking. He handed him the basket and walked away. Jude looked at his watch and gulped. The face read: air-slip complete! Want to do another?"

He must have slipped the recording code to this random Five server. Damnit, damnit, damnit. He only had one copy of the code left. He went in with the mission of slipping spy software to three major players: the head of Societal Efficiency, the president of

Inter-Tier Relations, and the director of the Purification Division. The best he could hope for now was getting out of here with just one of those watches bugged.

He summoned the courage he used when he jumped to what he thought would be his death on the bridge. Instead of overthinking it, he marched up to the director of the Purification Division—whom Samara thought was probably the most high-ranking—and slowly reached in the basket with the pair of tongs. He pinched a Kaiser roll with them, and then slowly lowered it onto the director's plate. A quick eye on his watch confirmed that the software had been slipped. The director didn't seem to have an alarm installed, and he seemed much more interested in his bread than he was in Jude. Relief swirled in Jude's chest. He was finally out of codes.

In order to avoid any more suspicion, he served Kaiser rolls to the rest of the table, rapid as a rush-hour barista, and then hustled back into the kitchen.

"I give the go-ahead to serve," said the kitchen manager. "Next time, you wait for me!"

Jude nodded, remembering the rules back home: do not speak unless absolutely necessary.

As promised, Jude went back into the bathroom. The server had dragged Davidson out of the stall and onto the bathroom floor.

"I thought he was dead," he said.

"He's not, is he?" asked Jude.

"No, he's breathing. But if he had been dead, I didn't want him to be slumped over a toilet. I didn't want his family to have to read that that's how they found him."

"You thought I'd killed him?"

"Yes."

Jude reached down to check for himself. He felt his pulse in his wrist and the side of his throat. He felt his chest come up and down. "Why do you trust me?"

"I'm a Five. I've only been told what to do, where to go, and when. I wish it wasn't this way, but trusting is as natural as breathing now. When the relocation happened and we all got knocked down to Unregistered status, most of us saw the writing on the wall and wondered when the higher tiers thought we were just leeches too. I guess I need someone to trust."

CHAPTER TWENTY-NINE

DENVER'S STOMACH TWISTED AS SHE SAT CROSS-LEGGED ON THE hotel bed and glared at the projected screens in front of her. She'd taken off her watch and set it on the nightstand beside the bed, which had dozens of old water rings scattered along the top. Her eyes darted from the actual footage of the bathroom, which showed a random waiter dragging the first target out of the bathroom stall (she was going to kill Jude for not just knocking him out, too) to the fake footage of the empty bathroom, to the banquet hall video, to the heat maps that more accurately showed Jude moving around the hotel. She saw that he'd gotten close enough to the Director of Societal Purification to air-slip, but if he'd found another opportunity to slip to the third target, she didn't see it. Jude had turned this mission into another bona fide disaster, but at least they were both still in one piece. She was still going to let him have it when he got back. When he left, she practiced her speech in her head, as she wanted to properly drive home the point that he was a major disappointment.

There was a knock at the door. It could be Jude, but she prepared for the possibility that it was not by closing all windows and activating a recording on her own watch that would broadcast back to Bristol and Samara back home. If she was about to have her final moments, she wanted them to have the option of knowing what happened. She opened the door without unlatching the chain-lock.

It was not Jude.

It was the Bird.

He was an old man, the oldest man Denver had ever seen before. Metrics guided people through death starting at age sixty, starting with pamphlets and seminars about what would happen when they took that final trip to the City Courthouse on their seventy-fifth birthday, so most people had a good fifteen years to prepare for the end. But the end had never come for this man. She had no idea how old he was, but it had to be at least a decade beyond the usual death age. There was not a fraction of an inch on his face that was not creased, folded, or puckered. He had no hair on his head, but plenty growing out of his ears. She'd seen old people in the UK, ones wearing the same kind of navy raincoats and matching track pants, as he did now, but none who looked like her. Though they had coordinated on the last mission through the military and the intelligence agencies, they hadn't the luxury of speaking beforehand about this one. She no longer had access to his contact information, and he had done a fantastic job at hiding it. Stephen probably could have reached out—he probably would have memorized his information, just in case—but Denver hadn't been practiced at that level of foresight at the time.

She wanted to smile, but her mouth would not obey. Her heart, beating fast, was too focused on what could still go wrong. Maybe his was too, because he did not smile either.

In a fluid motion, she shut the door, unlocked the chain, and opened it again just wide enough for him to get inside. For an old man, he was not frail. He was built like her brother, short and stocky.

He cleared his throat, a wet sound. "My condolences," he said, his voice rumbling a bit. "I never met your husband face-to-face, but I had many discussions with him. He was bright and a good man."

"Thank you."

He brought a cloth handkerchief to his lips and coughed again. This time, even behind the handkerchief, he did smile. "You don't seem pleased to see me."

"I am! I'm just wondering..."

"How I knew you were here? Your friend Daniel told me. Don't worry, the rest of the Red Sea doesn't know. He seemed to be wise enough to memorize one of my ID numbers the one time he saw it. He's with your brother right now in London. He wanted to be there in case—"

"In case we don't come back?" Denver flicked her hand out as if flicking a sheet, and her watch shot out projections of the screens she had just closed. "Definitely possible. I'm glad he thought of that."

"Your chances look pretty good to me," said the Bird. "Which one is Jude?"

Denver pointed to a little yellow dot on the screen.

"Ah," he said. "He's almost here. May I wait here for him? There are things I'd like to tell the two of you together. But for you, I have some good news and some bad news."

Denver nodded. He pulled up a chair from the little desk. "Bad news first, I'm afraid." He projected a picture from where he sat. She immediately recognized it as a mug shot—Metrics regularly projected these in public places with their ID numbers and citizenship scores below, which were always dismal, but this one was the only one she'd ever seen displayed in negative numbers. She didn't immediately recognize the woman in the picture, but once she did, she couldn't look away.

"Mom!" She gasped and looked back down at the citizenship score. She never thought what would happen if the citizenship score got to zero. She never thought it was possible.

"She's still alive," he said, "because Metrics' plan did not work out. They underestimated the amount of menial labor that still needs to be done. Coders insisted that they'd be able to build upon their systems to compensate, but they haven't been able to yet. They apprehended all the people connected to anyone with an escaped Unreg to help with labor needs."

Denver thought of Maureen, her friend who wasn't quite a friend, in marriage class all those years ago. She'd been the only other previous Three there in the Four class, but she and her husband were downgraded based on their citizenship scores because they were connected to people who'd been revolutionaries. They hadn't known. If what he was saying was true, Maureen and her husband were probably also in jail because of her.

Denver closed her eyes lightly. "My mother is still alive. You know this for sure?"

"I am still allowed a certain amount of privilege. I can tell you with almost certainty that she is. And if you and Jude and the rest of the world are successful at liberating this country, then she will be released."

"How can you be sure of that?"

"If the primary concern is human rights, they will be the first to be protected by the international community."

Jude walked in the room, breathless. He froze when he saw the Bird.

"Come in, young man. You've got the right room."

Jude walked in tentatively and took his place beside Denver. The old man smiled. "I'm not going to bite."

"We like standing," said Jude.

The Bird nodded. "I can understand why you wouldn't trust me. Why would you? I was a part of the team who put this whole system together. They call me one of the new founding fathers! But I'm also called the Bird. Do you know why?"

"Because during one of your speeches, you talked about how birds must be pushed out of the nest before they know they can fly."

"That's right," he said. "But that's often misinterpreted.

Metrics uses those words to tell the people that they have to be the ones to do the pushing. That if it weren't for them and the data on our citizens they gather from the time they are born, no one would be able to unlock his or her potential. But that was never what I meant by the speech. And maybe that was my fault. When we're not clear, our own words can be used against us easily, as mine were. Do you know what I meant to say?"

Denver felt like a child in the middle of a lecture, but she shook her head anyway. Beside her, Jude shook his.

"I meant that we are capable of more than we think we are. When we created Metrics, people were deeply unhappy with the status quo. People too busy to enjoy their lives. Many spent the whole of their young lives wasting their time wondering what the next ten years would bring them. People were divided, terribly divided, about race and religion. We thought the answer was as simple as taking away their problems. We were young ourselves and much too sure of ourselves. When I made that speech, I was talking to a group of future lawmakers who didn't know if they had what it took to completely overhaul a country, from culture to policy to values. We did."

"And you made a mess of it," said Denver.

"Yes, we did that too. The way we underestimated ourselves was nothing compared to how we underestimated others, particularly the poor. Underestimating the poor is a mistake all classes make, but it's a common trap. Social status is much easier and faster to see than character.

"My point is that we did actually overhaul the country. Nobody thought it was realistic—at times, not even us—but we are capable of much more than we believe. You are, too. Now, this country, as you aptly observed, my dear, is a mess. You did not ask for the burden of fixing it, yet it falls on you to do what needs to be done."

Denver felt her stomach turn to iron. She thought of the promise she'd made herself when the man at the bus stop had seen her as another leech on his tax dollars, and she longed, if only for

Stephen's sake, to spend the rest of her time here furthering his mission to make the world free.

Jude sagged. "Sir? We can't. I'm sorry, Denver, but I flopped on two bugs and only managed to install one copy of the code in the Societal Purity director's watch."

"It's okay, Jude," said Denver.

Jude stared at her with incredulous eyes.

"He's right. We'll go back to the UK with only one bug planted, and we'll work with whatever we can get."

"Hang on," said the Bird and waved his hand over his watch, frowning. "Is this report correct? This indicated that two copies were installed."

"Yeah, but I accidentally got too close to one of the servers and air-slipped it to him. He's just a Five."

The Bird grinned at Denver.

"I won't," said Denver.

"You won't what?"

"I won't make your mistake," said Denver. "I won't underestimate the poor."

"Good." The bird stood and smoothed his nylon pants. "In that case, it seems your work here is done. Come with me. I have a driverless transport. We'll make one stop, then my private airship can take you back home."

"Home?"

"It's a relative term, I know," said the Bird. "But in this case, I meant London. One day, I do hope that you are able to choose your home from anywhere in the world. Then, when someone says they're lending you their private airship to take you there, your reaction can be a bit happier than this."

If Denver had been a little younger and a little more naive, she would have hugged him. But this man was complicated; neither black nor white, neither good nor evil, neither humane nor monstrous. She wanted to hold someone responsible for the loss of her father, the hunt for her brother, the imprisonment of her mother, and the death of her husband, and though he didn't seem innocent, he did not seem like the one to blame either. She reached out her hand and gave him a firm handshake. Jude just nodded at him. Denver picked up her backpack and swung it onto her shoulders.

"We're ready."

CHAPTER THIRTY

JUDE'S STOMACH TURNED WHEN THEY MADE THEIR "ONE STOP." The vehicle turned into the Fox County Detention Center.

He considered letting Denver and the Bird go in alone while he waited out in the car, sure he wouldn't be able to handle the sights, or the sounds, or the putrid scents of the place he'd been incarcerated. But he didn't want to get separated again and compromise the whole mission. Denver and the Bird got out, but he hesitated.

"What?" asked Denver.

Jude looked up at the looming building, concrete and pale and cold. From the outside, it looked as if it were made of ice. "Nothing. Let's go."

They walked the halls, the guards nodding in deferment to the Bird. Jude recognized all of them, although there were fewer of them now, but they didn't give Jude a second glance. Jude had forgotten about that part of living here—you couldn't afford to be curious. Curiosity simply wasn't worth the price.

"I think our prisoner we've come to collect is over this way," said the Bird, tapping his watch. "Second floor?"

They walked through a hall of glass-plated cells, where the prisoners were just getting ready for lights out. The prisoners outnumbered the guards vastly. Jude remembered this from his time here, but the ratio was even more lopsided now.

He tried to do a quick estimation of that ratio in his head, and was so distracted that he almost walked past her.

Almost.

When he realized who it was, he froze mid-step. He turned without thinking, and there she was, behind glass, looking right at him, standing at attention as if she'd been waiting. She smirked and strode straight up to the small circle of holes in the glass, so he could hear her. "Reeder."

He couldn't quite believe his eyes. "Warden Paul?"

"They told me that you escaped."

"I..."

"They told me that I was to blame. They came with strong men and they carried me from my office to this cell. They held me down and they put a tracking chip in my hand."

The Bird came back for him, pressing a hand on Jude's shoulder. Warden Paul's face shot up at him. "You found him?" she asked.

"We got him," said the Bird.

"I'm free?"

"Your case will be reviewed," said the Bird, and Jude's stomach turned. It was so strange. Though Warden Paul had tried to kill him and almost succeeded, she was a pitiful sight now. Her hair hung in strings along her hollowed-out cheeks, and she was the color of the split pea soup they used to serve here. Her eyes, once sweeping and scanning, making sure every corner was tucked and each prisoner standing erect in her presence, now turned to Jude, feral and bloodshot.

"I knew it," she said and pressed both of her hands to the glass as the Bird led him away. "I knew it! Justice always prevails!"

They increased their pace, and Jude covertly dodged the Bird when he made a motion to put his arm around his shoulder. "Why'd you tell her that?" he asked quietly.

"Governing 101, son," he said, rounding a corner. "They all need hope."

CHAPTER THIRTY-ONE

SAMARA CRACKED TWO EGGS. SHE WAS TRYING TO BE MORE mindful of doing these little things so that, hopefully, the same mindfulness would carry into her work at the library. As hard as she worked to understand every line of the UK's body politic, she struggled. These laws weren't written with the goal of common folk like her to be able to use it to their advantage.

She heard a noise coming from behind her and hurriedly dumped the eggs into the pan, mindfulness be damned. There was another reason she spent all of her time at the library now—she was avoiding Bristol. Just at the moment she knew she was in love with him and would be forever, she promptly grew terrified of him as well. They were living in close quarters, and he worked from home, so she had to be creative if she was to be sure they would not see each other. She woke early. She slipped in late. She spent hours outside and in public buildings, not spending any money, which she knew was really his, if she didn't really have to. He'd asked her a long time ago to get married, which she thought may be impossible now for good. Sharing that much of your life with someone almost certainly meant sharing the details of her assault, and she never wanted to think about that ever again.

What was he doing up this early? She gingerly took a plate from the stack in the cupboard, but her fingers slipped and the plate shattered with the loudest explosion on the floor. She gritted her teeth, turned off the heat from the stove, and grabbed the broom and dustpan.

Bristol emerged in the doorway wearing shorts and a plain white T-shirt. "Are you okay?" he asked.

"I'm fine. Dropped a plate. I hope it wasn't valuable."

"Not at all. Let me help."

"I've got it. Go back to bed."

Bristol kneeled down and took the dustpan from her. "I'll just hold this still," he said. Samara held her breath as she swept the broken blue pieces into the pan. "I haven't seen you hardly at all since you got here."

"I've been busy. I'm still busy, actually, so if you wouldn't mind—"

"Tell me about your work. Albert says you go to the library."

Samara sighed. It didn't seem to matter how he knew. "I'm trying to find a way we can use the constitution to our advantage. Metrics has a simple document that lots of people interpret. The UK doesn't have anything like that—their constitution is a stack of papers a mile long that summarizes every kind of law imaginable, and books by constitutional law experts. It's awful. There are precedents for refugees being allowed temporary sanctuary status when their home countries are experiencing war, but not in the UK. And it's not war that's happening back home, it's a massacre. I have new ideas every day, and I try to keep my hope up, but by the end of the day each one seems more and more unlikely."

"You'll find something."

"I'm grasping and getting nowhere. I'm worried that once Denver and Jude get back with the proof and you unveil your new painting and we embarrass Metrics by baiting them into bidding on it, we'll still have no foundation for staying here. Metrics will kill us on the spot if we're sent back, and the UK will know just where to find us."

"Why don't I come with you today? I need a break."

"You need to finish."

"I'm almost done. And I'm serious, I can't look at that canvas anymore. Nothing about it makes sense to me anymore, and it won't unless I get some air."

Samara wanted to tell him that the library was the last place that he wanted to look if he wanted to get some air, but she held her tongue and nodded. If he were Taye, he'd spend about ten minutes with her before getting bored and making some excuse to get away. What scared her about Bristol was that he'd actually stay with her as long as she could stay at the library, which spanned the entirety of their open hours.

In the grand reading room, it took Samara the better part of an hour to get into a concentration groove, and even longer to focus enough to actually research. She gave Bristol little jobs, like book-fetching and fact-checking and footnote-digging, and he did her bidding with no questions asked.

Eventually, he insisted on a lunch break and took her to the pub across the street. The day outside was bright and sunny, but the pub was as dark as the drab paint that adorned every surface: olive greens, chocolate browns, navy blues, and no windows anywhere that weren't stained glass. He ordered fish and chips for both of them, as well as a cider for himself. "Anything for you?" he asked.

She shook her head.

"Have you tried cider yet? I think you'd like it."

"Of course I've tried it."

"You don't like it? I thought everybody liked it. It's fizzy apple juice, what's not to like?"

"It's not that."

Bristol leaned over his crossed arms on the bar. "It's our money. All of us have worked for it, and there's plenty of it."

"There's plenty of it now, but it goes so fast. And we have not all worked for it. You're the one who made the art that sold. I just spin my wheels all day."

"You're getting closer to an answer for us." He held up two fingers to the bartender, who poured another pint for Samara. She added the amount to the tally in her head; after that, she might as well enjoy it.

"There's something different about you," said Bristol.

"Astute observation."

"I'm sorry. That was insensitive. I just mean that in all the years I've known you, I've never seen you work like this before. You were always more...deliberate before. Much slower. Now you're a little more..."

"Frantic. Hysterical. Hair-brained. You really know the way to a girl's heart"

"I wish I did," said Bristol. "Have you tried...I don't know, slowing down? I'm doing that now with this piece and even though it's counterintuitive, it's actually taking me less time even though I'm moving slower. I'm having to go back and fix less. Maybe take a day off, clear your mind."

"That's hard for me to do," said Samara. "The world used to be a good place for me. It's gradually gotten more and more terrifying. If I stop thinking a second about finding an iron-clad reason the Brits have to let us stay, I start thinking about Metrics and being sent back. If I stop thinking about being sent back, I start thinking about Stephen. If I stop thinking about Stephen, I start thinking about men and how they violate women."

"And from there, everything spirals," Bristol finished for her. He took a sip of his cider and pushed hers an inch closer to her. He changed the subject to everyone's favorite here—the weather— and the two of them ate their fish and chips in peace, interrupted only by football commentary on the old TVs above the bar. When it was time to go back to the library, Samara looked down while Bristol paid the bill.

Though most people paid with their thumbprints or watches, Bristol now carried cash. He put some notes down, and handed some to Samara. "You haven't been taking enough from the lockbox. I don't know how you're eating."

Samara tried to hand it back. "I eat the groceries in the apartment."

"Before the sun rises and after the sun sets?"

"I usually take an apple and granola bar too."

"We've had enough food in bar form to last a lifetime. This city isn't exactly known for its culinary delicacies, but if you really try, you can find better food than what we had at the warehouse or Olympic Village or St. Mary's." Bristol grinned, but his eyes stayed sad.

"I don't deserve—"

"You know that none of this is your fault, right? None of it. You're not weak and you never were. In fact, you're so much stronger now than ever."

"How can that be true? Things keep happening to me. I haven't made anything happen for me."

"How about sacrificing yourself for me and Jude? How about reorganizing our camp to keep the entire group safe? How about putting your attacker behind bars? You've made a lot happen, Samara. And in every case, you know how you did it. You're not giving yourself credit."

"I don't know. I guess in every example you just said, the answer just kind of...came to me. I just got lucky."

"You allowed yourself to think clearly and you came to the right solution. You can do it again. I agree that we need a backup in case all other plans fail."

As much as she preferred to work as she had been, she could see the wisdom in Bristol's suggestion. "I'll need some time alone, then."

Bristol groaned. "More alone time? You sure you don't want a little company?"

"You don't think less of me now?"

"What? No. No, no, no, no. I can't—I wouldn't—" He stopped to half-laugh. "Samara, you think you're broken, but you are the opposite of broken. I've always thought highly of you, but after what you've been though...To me, you're heaven."

Samara thought back to four years earlier, when she'd kissed him in Nan's kitchen. She was sure he had feelings for her, but she didn't need any drawn-out confessions of love before she took action. Here, she felt as muted and dingy as the pub she sat in, an unnoticed accouterment, quietly gathering dust as the decades rolled by. She wanted to communicate this, but as she gathered the remaining bits of her courage to tell him that she was no longer good enough, he reached out, held her head, thumbs on her temples, and kissed the center of her forehead. She leaned into him, and the lean turned into a hug, and the hug turned into tears into his chest.

"I know you're probably not thinking about love right now," he said, his breath warm next to her ear. "But just know that I'm here for you. There's no one else for me but you."

"Get a room!" The bartender, who'd been engrossed in the football game this entire time, had suddenly taken an interest them. They jumped and bolted apart.

Samara didn't quite laugh, but she felt laughter's familiar rumblings in her chest. "You know? We just might."

CHAPTER THIRTY-TWO

BRISTOL DID NOT WORK ON THE PIECE THAT AFTERNOON.

Or the rest of the day.

He and Samara did check in with Daniel eventually, who, perhaps sensing the two needed some space, had asked to stay with another friend in the city. Denver and Jude were on their way back and would be on this side of the Atlantic by midnight. Already the intelligence they'd gathered was pretty damning on the part of Metrics—and Daniel assured them that the Red Sea would take their case back to Parliament to prove that they were planning another massacre.

Later, the three of them went to a dark airfield, where every star was visible against the velvet night. Though summer was just around the corner, they bundled themselves in layers against the cold and watched the sky in silence. Bristol breathed in the crisp air. How many more chances would he have to do that? Being so close to death so many times had a strange effect on how he lived his life. A part of him felt invincible, as if so many brushes and misses rendered him untouchable. Another part clung to life in strange ways. Making sure to enjoy every meal, smell every flower, say what he meant. He'd had the experience of being without oxygen before and, somehow, his body remembered. Beside him, Samara took an equally long breath in and out, matching him. Maybe hers remembered too.

In the distance, a light wavered. He squinted. Were his eyes getting older? Worse? He stared at it until he was sure it wasn't just another star. On his other side, Daniel said in his hushed baritone, "Well, there they are."

The airship was tiny compared to commercial ones, blacker than the night sky and much shinier. Bristol held his breath as it landed, hovering just above the ground for a moment before touching down lightly. He prayed that his sister and friend were the only two who would get out.

The door lifted, and for a moment, there was no one. Bristol stepped forward in front of Samara and Daniel, deepening his stance. Then a tall, thin woman with no hair stepped out, followed by a gangly teenage boy's frame.

Bristol and Samara ran for them. When Bristol had the three of them locked in a hug, he smiled so hard he felt his mouth might spring from his face. They laughed until they cried, or maybe the other way around. Daniel met them and wrapped his giant arms around the four, lifted them all, and made the laughter even more uncontrollable. Bristol realized Denver was trying to say something through the spasms.

"What?" asked Bristol.

"I said...I said..." She wiped tears with her fingertips. "We never have to go back. We never have to go back again."

Bristol looked at her for a moment and closed his mouth. What did she mean by that? They did eventually have to go back, if nothing else to find out what happened to...

He whipped around to look back at the airship. She was standing there, waiting for him to notice her.

"Mom!"

He yelled into the light beam from the plane, a heart sound that he'd never heard anyone make before. He ran and embraced her. Under the temporary airship scent, she smelled the same.

Cool. Fresh linen and peppermint. "How?" He turned to his sister. "How?"

"You tell him," their mother told Denver. "I'm not even sure I understand it."

"Metrics had put her in prison."

"Prison? Wasn't the point of the relocation to get rid of those?"

"The relocation had some unintended consequences," said Denver. "They found that they needed some Unregs after all. We met the Bird, and he pulled strings—that man is a great hacker for his age—and a guard brought Mom out and shoved her into our transport."

"I thought I was...going to see you," said Mom, cradling Bristol's jaw in the palms of her hands. "But not like this. Are we really alive?"

Bristol's tears were heavy and fell straight from his cheeks to the ground. "We are. I'm alive. You're alive."

"It's a miracle. We all made it."

From the corner of his eye, he saw Denver bow her head. He clasped her shoulder. "What's next?"

"I assume we have a transport to take us back to the apartment. I'll tell you more when we're home, okay?"

Daniel, tight-jawed, flung a gesture toward a long white van with tinted windows. "Fifteen-passenger! We'll all be comfortable. It needs a driver, but I can do it if you want to catch up."

"Are you okay, Daniel?" asked Bristol.

"Fine. Fine."

"What is it?" asked Jude.

Daniel broke into loud sobs. "Yer mother! Alive! Yesterday she was in prison an' she thought her children were dead an' now yer all together again! It's...it's...enough to make a man patriotic!"

Denver looked disgusted, but mostly in a bewildered sense. "Pull yourself together. And never say the P word around us again."

"Yeah," said Bristol, punching his shoulder softly with one hand while holding his mother's with the other. "Stranger things have happened, you know."

Daniel blew his nose into his sleeve. "Away an shite, ya numpties." He jerked and looked pointedly at Mrs. Ray. "Sorry, ma'am."

"I have no idea what he just said," she said to her son.

"It takes a while for your ears to get used to it," he said.

"Basically, he told us to go take a poop and insulted our intelligence." Denver picked up her backpack and crossed the field to the van, picking up her feet so her socks stayed dry in the tall grass. "I think it's a phrase to indicate endearment, but who knows?"

"It might be," said Daniel, who smiled at Denver's marching. "But I won't admit it."

Daniel and Mrs. Ray chatted the entire way home from the driver's and passenger's seat, but she still stretched her shoulder to hold Bristol's hand from the next row. Occasionally, she asked for a translation, which Bristol provided. He was surprised that he was even able to offer this since it didn't seem so long ago when he himself had trouble understanding the accented English. He kept looking at her hand—the hand that had pulled his body close to hers when he was born. It looked much the same as it always had—broad palm, long fingers, close in length—but drier than he'd ever seen it.

"Didja drink much water on the plane?" asked Bristol.

On his left side, Denver nodded knowingly. "As much as we could," she said. She leaned in and whispered, "Look at her pinky finger."

He looked.

There was no nail. Instead, there was a dry black scab at the end of her finger. His mother seemed to feel him looking and turned around. "It didn't hurt."

"They pulled out your fingernail?"

"I'd had enough, Bristol. They were abusing one of my cell mates. A girl just one year younger than Denver. I couldn't have that. The guard came in—"

"A male guard?" Samara asked.

"Yes. He came in, and I could tell he was going to do it again, what he did every night. I told him his mother would be ashamed. He ignored me. I don't even think he heard me, but then they called me into an interrogation room the next day and had me look at pictures of the two of you. Told me all these lies about you. Said I needed to be punished for raising two worthless children, and slowly pulled out both nails on my little fingers. They had these recordings of you both that they kept playing."

Bristol could not look up. "What did we say? On the recordings?"

"Den's watch must have not been lit, but they recorded anyway. Some things about you sneaking away at night, Bristol. Lots of 'don't tell Mom' or 'stop before she finds out.'"

Denver and Bristol exchanged glances. He should have known that Metrics would use those watches to spy on them. They'd been naive to think that recordings only happened when it flashed the blue warning light.

Back at the apartment, Bristol and Samara made tea and served it to the others while they were curled on couches in the little living room. It was a bit sparse, with only one loveseat and a rocking chair, but most of them spread out on the large olive green and gold Turkish rug on the floor. Bristol turned on a lamp from the side table while Samara handed out steaming mugs. Bristol took in his mother's face as she looked up in appreciation to Samara. She brought the mug to her nose and sniffed.

"What is this?" she asked.

"Chamomile," said Samara. "It should help you sleep."

Mom took a sip. "Probably need all the help I can get. I'm so tired it feels like I won't sleep for days. Or maybe I'm so excited that I'll pass out before my head hits the pillow. Anyway, I guess chamomile can't hurt." She stood. "Actually, I'm a little restless. You stay here, I'm going to take myself on a little tour of your home."

She stood and poked her head around the hallway. She opened

the closet, saw Bristol's coat flung on the floor, picked it up, and hung it on the hanger.

"I can get that, Mom," said Bristol, reaching for it.

"I'm just happy I get to do anything for you, sweetheart. What's in here?"

"My room. It's yours tonight."

"Don't mind if I do." She meandered inside, seeming to take note of everything: the deodorant on his dresser, the change on his nightstand, the book face down like a tent on the bed. He knew it was a matter of time before she'd pause in front of the drawing. He didn't necessarily want to be here for that. He stepped back out into the doorway, which opened back into the living room.

"So how did it go?" Samara asked Denver.

Denver and Jude exchanged a smile, the first Bristol had ever seen between the two. "Well," she said. "Awfully well."

CHAPTER THIRTY-THREE

JUDE SIPPED HIS TEA WHILE DENVER TOLD THE ROOM OF THE initial findings of the recordings. Then, anticipating that they'd want to hear some for themselves, he tapped his watch face and played them a chilling soundbite from the Director of Societal Purity:

We had to remove the Unregistered from the society. The "relocation," as the public refers to it, was extremely successful. Not only did we succeed in creating more room and resources for the people who matter, we did it without the public knowing that we sacrificed over a million lives, and we disposed of the bodies quickly and efficiently. Now that we know how to do it, we can repeat the process with the Fives, and we can do it better than before. We can anticipate problems. One of the big consequences our researches missed was the overestimation of machine capability to do menial work. It seems that we do need to imprison about ten percent of the Fives to meet demand, but we do not need all of them, and once machine capability reaches maximum efficiency, we can get rid of the entirety of the prison population, as planned.

There was a thunderous round of applause after that clip.

"He said that in a meeting. We know from prior conversations that there were well over a hundred people in the room." Jude sniffed. He felt a cold coming on. He breathed in the steam from his cup. "They're pretty shameless about it. They knew there'd be no Fives in the room, or anyone who'd allow themselves to be associated with a Five."

"Because they have new citizenship score criteria, they had to implement new limits so more people would be incarcerated," said Denver. "We thought relations between tiers were bad when we were there, but it was nothing like it is now. People wouldn't dream of associating with a lower tier in any way. Even when they're picking up groceries or tipping their drivers, no words are exchanged to avoid suspicion."

Samara shook her head. "Insanity."

"It's progress that you think that," said Jude. "I really thought I'd broken out of the whole Metrics mindset, but being back made me feel...back. There again, with all that pressure to succeed. I never wanted to abort the mission, but Metrics just has a way of making you feel...safe, if you side with them. People are spying on each other now in order to raise their score or lower their neighbor's. I know it was always that way, but it's intensified now."

"So even though it's not going to be totally easy to convince the international community that they should liberate the United States, it's going to be much harder to liberate the people under Metrics from their own mindsets," Denver said.

"But Metrics is killing people," Samara said.

"You don't understand. The director said what he said in a huge, crowded room. And we have some audio from a random Five, too. They're aware of the plan as well. They're just choosing to believe that they will actually be relocated, as opposed to murdered like the Unregistered. They think if they side with Metrics, all will be well." Jude reached for a tissue and blotted his nose. "I had that same feeling. I thought for sure that Metrics would see that I was innocent and release me from the detention center. I wouldn't have imagined that they put me there in the first place."

"And I almost turned Stephen in for being associated with the

Red Sea, even though I knew Metrics had set us up in hopes to spy on us both," said Denver through an ironic smile. "Human beings are so bizarre! It's as if they take away our common sense."

"Or we willingly give it away," said Jude. "So where do we go from here? Daniel?"

Daniel hadn't moved from his position, seated next to Denver on the loveseat with a deep lean forward and his thick forearms rested on his knees. "I'll take the recordings back to the Red Sea. They can set up a meeting with the United Countries. I'm guessing they'll change your status back to refugee and then from there it's all politics. That's where Bristol comes in, changing public opinion."

Samara turned to Bristol. "Show them what you've been working on."

Bristol turned his head toward his room and said, "That's it." His mother came out with a medium-sized canvas, holding it in front of her as if it were made of crystal.

As far as first impressions go, Jude was a little underwhelmed. Not that he knew much about art, but most of Bristol's work looked pretty cool—vibrant colors with stark contrasts, realistic detail, thought-provoking themes. If this was really it, it sucked. A few black figures on a small, dirty-looking canvas. This was supposed to be a piece that was more than what it was. He knew Bristol didn't like asking his art to be anything more than art, but after what he'd been through, this seemed a little insulting.

Apparently Denver was thinking along the same lines. "What is that?"

"Anything can be pretty immediately and fade out," said Bristol. "I wanted this one to be a little more lasting." He explained his mediums. Jude actually gasped when he told them about the charcoal.

"Jesus, Bristol, they're going to think we're serial killers or something." Jude scrubbed at his face with his fingers, feeling the effects of exhaustion slowly sink into his skull. "I don't want you to think I'm being critical, but—"

"—but that's not what we need and you know it." Denver finished.

Bristol frowned and jerked his head back. "Big has been done, though. Color has been done. This has not been done."

"Yeah, I think art people will understand that." Denver moved her hand as if to flip her hair, but her hand just flew through the air. She didn't seem concerned. "They'll probably give your little arts and crafts project here four Michelin stars or something. Two thumbs up, ten tomatoes, whatever."

"But it's a matter of convincing the public, too." Samara nodded. "I think she has a point. On its own, it's not powerful enough unless you know the story. It doesn't quite speak for itself."

"Then let it speak," said Bristol and Denver's mother. Jude glanced from the canvas to her face. She was staring straight at Jude, and she wasn't smiling. He searched her for a moment, but wheels in his mind were turning painfully slow.

Bristol, after a second, said, "I like it." He looked at Jude. "Can we do that?"

Jude felt so dumb. "Do what?"

"Can we use the audio recordings to make this a multimedia piece in the slow? We can add a sound cone over it, so when people walk up to it to look, they can hear the clip you just played."

"That'd be perfect," said Denver. "We should add the voice of the Five in, too. The Bird told us not to underestimate the poor. Albert will know the people to set up a show. We'll have Cindy set up an exhibition in Edinburgh, too. Daniel, you check on the Red Sea efforts first, and we'll get moving on that right after they know."

Daniel winked. "You're the boss."

Jude would have skipped the wink, but otherwise, he thought it was the perfect way to describe her.

Jude's body woke him early and refused to let him sleep anymore. It wasn't that the floor was uncomfortable—he was used to that—it was the patch of sunlight shining on his cheek. It was warm and gentle, like a kiss. He'd never actually been kissed, not even, as far as he knew, by his mother, but he'd seen the deed done and thought it might be nice.

He wondered where Cork was and what he was doing at this moment. Was he inside or outside? Hungry or satisfied? Warm or chilly? Sleeping or awake? If they were still at the warehouse together, they'd already be on the floor, toting boxes of things people didn't need into bins where they'd be brought to them. It seemed an entire lifetime had passed since they'd worked together, making little inside jokes as they passed each other and then staying up late at night to whisper to each other about anything, anything at all, as long as it wasn't strategy. He'd been hoping, for years, to finally have worked hard enough to not have to specifically avoid this topic in future conversations. To talk about football as the entire point of the conversation and not feel like they were skating on ice over an angry rushing river.

He got up, folded his blanket, and draped it over the loveseat where Samara slept, snoring softly though her nose. He went into the kitchen and filled the kettle for tea. Mrs. Ray was standing outside on the little balcony off the kitchen. He bowed his head as he turned on the gas, hoping to avoid her, but she saw him, opened the door, and enveloped him in hug.

"Good morning, honey," she said. "Couldn't sleep either?"

"I'm just an early riser, I guess."

She opened the cabinet and got out a mug for him. "You know what they say about the early bird."

He blinked. "What?"

Smiling, but with a quizzical brow she answered, "The early bird gets the worm. I guess it is an old expression. I guess your mother didn't say that much."

He shook his head and stared at the mug. Though back at home he'd been a Two and Denver and Bristol's family had been

Threes, they'd grown up with so much privilege. In his former home, Jude would go downstairs in the morning to a sleek kitchen, sit under the marble bar, and tap his watch. The cuisine assembler would whir and buzz and wouldn't stop until eventually a high-pitched ding would signal that his oatmeal was done, complete with whole milk, fresh seasonal berries, and toasted walnuts. He'd eat it in silence, reviewing his homework on his watch. At times, his mother or even his father would come down and start the cuisine assembler for their own breakfast, but no words beyond "hello" were ever exchanged. She certainly never said any offhand, old-fashioned folksy phrases. The Twos were high society and kept busy with all sorts of obligations, both professional and social. She had her own life.

Mrs. Ray had her own life, too, but she made her children a part of it. Free of the high expectations, her family had been able to access a wealth that Jude's family had never known.

"No, but I think my mother probably knew it. She was always up early."

Mrs. Ray nodded and unlatched a large wooden box. "Bristol has so much tea here."

"His patron got him that as a gift. He thinks we ought to know more about tea than we do. None of our palates are refined enough for him."

She laughed. "He's in for a rude awakening then. If there's one thing I've learned, it's that trying to change people into whatever you think they should be only ends badly for you."

"Reminds me of Metrics." Jude picked out a bag of English breakfast—the only one in the entire box he'd even tried—and opened it.

"Me, too."

"This actually brings me to something I wanted to tell you," Mrs. Ray said.

"Me?"

"Yes. I know we don't know each other well yet, but I wanted to encourage you to...be yourself."

He hoped she didn't mean what he thought she meant, but her smile suggested it was exactly that. "What do you mean?" he asked.

"Denver told me about your feelings for Cork. My late husband was gay. Metrics thought that meant something was inherently wrong with him. His mind or his body or his lived experiences or something else they thought he should be able to control but wouldn't. I didn't find out until a year after we were married, and I'd already fallen in love with my neighbor. We didn't get to talk about it before I got pregnant with Denver. I think if we'd talked about it right away, he might still be here. But all the secrets and lies—from both of us—eventually broke him. He had to keep his true nature hidden from Metrics, then hidden from me, then hidden from our children. It was like he was imprisoned inside his own body. He didn't reach out to me much, but I suspect that there was a whole world inside his mind. He wrote me a letter the morning he stepped in front of the train and said he didn't kill himself because he was gay. He did it because he was too heartbroken to go on and he didn't think anyone would miss someone they didn't really know."

Her face was stone. "But I do miss him. I did love him, not romantically, but genuinely. The world would have been a better place if he was here." She squeezed his hand. "Not that you'd consider something like that, honey, but I wanted to tell you that your mind has a way of suffocating a person when they keep something like love to themselves. Love has to be shared. Love has to breathe."

"I...I can never be with Cork and both of us know it." Jude gulped. "I did something so stupid that all I want to do is forget about it. I want him to forget about me, too."

"Honey, doing stupid things is love's calling card."

"Not this stupid."

She reached out and touched his wrist. "You didn't do it on purpose. You didn't set out to hurt anyone."

Jude nodded, his chest tight. "I wanted to help. I really didn't think I could do it without him." He broke away from her hand to touch the corner of his eye. "Do you think Denver will ever forgive me?"

"She's getting closer. But you can't control her; that will be her choice. But if I know my daughter's heart, I know she wouldn't wish lost love on anyone."

Jude stood up. "I'm sorry, Mrs. Ray, but I think I need some air."

He walked down the steps and into the morning, where scents of freshly baked bread and rotting garbage swirled together and made him feel nauseous. He walked until he got to the river and remembered the jump. How the adrenaline had fueled it all, how his crushing guilt had driven him there. Mrs. Ray was right, but at the time, he was convinced that he was making the decision for other people. The truth was that he was selfishly trying to go backward. But people weren't made to go backward. Jude leaned over the railing and savored the feeling of the cool air off the river on his face. People were made to go forward.

CHAPTER THIRTY-FOUR

DENVER DECIDED TO GO TO THE RED SEA HEADQUARTERS WITH Daniel the next day. She wondered, on the way, whether or not it was a bad idea, since the office park on the outskirts had been a place that she and Stephen had gone to frequently. She hadn't been back since his death. But her exhaustion protected her from over analysis, and she sat on the subway car next to Daniel with no thoughts in her mind beyond the hope that the man who sat on the other side with the boiled eggs in his bag would get off at the next station.

He did. She chose to see that as a good omen and stood when they announced her station a few stops later. Her eyes, she knew, were puffy, her skin patchy without a chance to properly wash it. She wanted to get this done as soon as possible. The hand-off, the initial interrogation.

Red Sea Headquarters was just three floors of a bland looking office building, light brown walls below a deep brown roof. It only looked about fifty years old, but here, most buildings built in that era hadn't been designed to stand the test of time. There were some good things about Metrics—the lack of resources meant that most things were built to last, if only for a few tiers of people.

Here, weeds grew out from the edges of the foundation, cracks snaked through the pavement and, in front of the entrance, a large rubber welcome mat bid them "w-lc-m."

Stephen and Denver had met here for months to strategize on the plan to involve the top British spy agencies in hopes of getting evidence that Metrics had indeed killed the Unregistered and that they were willing to do it again. This morning, she would walk in with proof right there on her wrist, obtained without any support from them or the agencies they'd worked so hard to convince. She realized on the lift up that although she'd been too tired to feel most emotions this morning, she did feel proud of herself for that.

"Ready?"

Stephen would ask her the same question right before they went in.

"Always," said Denver automatically.

"What?" asked Daniel.

She turned to him. "You asked if I was ready."

"No, I didn't." The elevator dinged and the doors opened. Daniel walked out first. "You must be hearing things."

The back of Denver's neck prickled, but instead of feeling cold, there was a sudden warmth all over her. "Finally."

CHAPTER THIRTY-FIVE

"I'VE HAD AN IDEA."

Samara pulled a short book from her bag. It was red and old, but the protective library cover had preserved it somewhat, so its edges were light and the color gradually got deeper at the center. "Asylum was restricted in the UK over a hundred years ago because some refugees were inciting acts of violence in England, hoping to ignite some larger political turnover. Asylum was never a broad protection, but it became much narrower after that and hasn't expanded much since. The only reason it's so restricted was because it was never properly extended back after the threat had passed. If the UK and its allies decide to invade the US, then we'll be granted asylum, but for the rest of the refugees who aren't protected, they won't. They'll have to keep hiding in the factories and farms."

Bristol nodded. "You know what it makes me think of? Danovan. Remember when he suggested assassinating the far-right politicians who were telling people that the relocation never happened?"

"Yeah."

"I knew it was a bad idea, but I didn't stop and think that it

would set back causes for people who hadn't even been born yet."
He scratched the back of his head. "So what's your idea?"

"I always thought you had to be an elected official, or at least a
lawyer, to write laws. Turns out, you can be anyone. You just have
to get your law sponsored by a member of Parliament, who takes it
to the floor, votes, and then if it passes, it becomes a part of the
British constitution. Easy."

"Are you sure? Not that I have much experience, but I'm pretty
sure that exactly nothing involving Parliament is easy."

"Well, it's easier than impossible."

"So you're going to write a law?"

"Actually," she took stapled stack of papers from her bag, "I've
already written one. It's kind of messy, but I think once I can get
an attorney at the Red Sea to look it over, they can bring it to a
representative, who can bring it to Parliament."

Bristol smiled at her and gave her a quick, crisp kiss on the
cheek. "You're brilliant."

"I'm not the only one." The truth was that she didn't quite feel
brilliant, but she had put in the time, thinking and doing and not
avoiding shortcuts. And that made her feel even better somehow.
If she couldn't control her birthplace or citizenship status or, in
this moment, her education level, she could at least control how
she spent her time.

The Red Sea had a busy week. While they were revising
Samara's proposal and taking the recordings from Jude and
Denver to the international collective of allies, Samara helped
Bristol get ready for the art show. It was a solo exhibition.
Albert worked with a team of impeccably dressed people,
including Cindy, who'd taken the train as soon as she'd heard
that Bristol was still in the UK and very much alive. Samara had
been in the apartment when she'd come. She'd barreled into
Bristol, gripped him around his neck in a tight hug, and
whispered something Samara couldn't quite hear into his ear.
Bristol had been polite, but kept her at arm's length after that.
She didn't think he'd revealed anything about their relationship

—it was too soon for that, and she was clear that she didn't want to complicate any public perception with romance—but Cindy turned icy later that afternoon and her interactions with Samara were decidedly cold.

But Cindy was still good at her job. She'd still called in every favor, contacted everyone she knew in London. Albert and his team booked a hip little gallery that had a reputation for controversial installations, and arranged for most of his pieces to be shipped from Edinburgh. There was public buzz. The news that there were illegal immigrants in London was nothing new, but the news had publicized the Metrics recordings by then, and the political pundits were tracking the movement of Samara's law through Parliament. Their issue was already a media sensation, and though there hadn't been much time to publicize the show, the art community clearly wouldn't miss the chance to be a part of it.

The day tickets went on sale, they were putting final touches on lighting, moving around the pieces in a way that told their story. Cindy's watch buzzed while they were in the gallery. She grinned at Bristol, and it didn't fade even as her eyes passed over Samara. "Going to need more wine," she said.

"Sold out?" said Bristol, looking down at her wrist. "But this place is huge!"

Cindy laughed in that stupid way, several registers above her work voice. "Everyone wants to meet you!"

"But they can't," said Samara. Cindy's body went from light to heavy. Samara tried to make her voice a little more friendly. "Right? The bill relaxing the asylum laws hasn't gone through yet. He'd be a sitting duck for immigration police."

"Oh," said Cindy, twirling a piece of her nourished blonde hair, "I don't think they'd pick him up at his own show. This is the Circle House. Immigration officers aren't just going to barge in here and arrest him."

Samara wanted to tell her that she thought that because she didn't think it could happen to her, but she stopped herself. Privilege was in the way of her understanding, and a critique here in front of Bristol, however true, wasn't going to remove it. "Well," she said, "it's a gamble. Is it worth it to you, to risk deportation?"

Cindy narrowed her eyes and crossed one long leg over the other. "They won't come into an artist's reception."

"They might, Cindy," Bristol said. "I don't want to play this card, but we've been through a lot. Even if you think it's impossible, it's not worth even a one percent chance to me."

Cindy rolled her eyes. "We'll just have to amp up the mystery, then. Hype up the elusive American artist Bristol Ray. It's not ideal, but it's the next best thing to having you."

It was only a matter of minutes before a government official opened the unlocked front door and walked inside.

Samara's heart caught mid-beat initially, but she realized that she recognized him. One of Clara Clovinger's bodyguards. She hadn't seen him for months.

"Miss Shepherd," he said, his voice as low and dark as his sunglasses, which he kept on even though he was indoors.

"Hello."

Cindy whimpered.

"Miss Shepherd, I'm to take you to the Grand Arms Hotel. The first minister is waiting there to speak with you."

Samara and Bristol glanced at each other. What could this mean? Bristol asked the bodyguard if he could come along.

"No. I'm here to collect Miss Shepherd only." He glanced at his holowatch. "Now."

Samara went with him outside and slid into the shiny black limousine. The last time she'd ridden in this kind of transport, shiny and sophisticated and driverless, she was going to meet Clovinger for the first time. Today, she had the feeling it might be her last. Samara and the bodyguard faced each other in parallel park-bench-sized matte seats.

"Do you know what this is about?" asked Samara.

"Yes."

"Will you tell me?"

"No."

She hoped he saw the scowl on her lips and not the tremor in her jaw.

The car parked itself, and with more agility than she remembered, he leaped from the car and swooped to open her door for her. "Walk with me."

They walked into a golden lobby with a large fountain in the center under a crystal chandelier. The floor glittered with specks of silver among the shimmering tile, and exotic plants were placed strategically among the walls. *This can't be bad news*, she thought. *Why would Clovinger bring me here to give me bad news?* But then she remembered Cindy and how she was so confident, despite everything she knew they'd been though, that the police wouldn't dare arrest them at an art show. Ritzy or not, there was no reason she couldn't be arrested here either.

In the elevator, they went up so high that Samara had to swallow several times to pop her ears. She watched the little numbers light as the elevator moved past the floors. 44...45...46...

When the elevator finally stopped, the doors did not open. The bodyguard placed his thumb on a sensor pad, where a green laser read his prints. "Lift opens to the suite," he said. "By the way, you have something in your teeth."

Samara's hand flew to her mouth. "You couldn't have hold me before now?"

"Kidding."

She wanted to tell him it wasn't funny, but then again, maybe it was. Unless he was about to arrest her.

The doors opened on an airy room with pale yellow furniture and long white drapes over the windows. The windows were cracked open, so the drapes danced, but with a bit of reservation.

"Wait here, please. Would you like a glass of water?"

"No, thank you." Samara tried to remember how to appear in front of the first minister. Sit straight. Ankles crossed. Something still seemed off, but maybe that was because she hadn't practiced in a while.

Clovinger's steps rang out from the short hallway, and Samara jumped to her feet the moment she heard her. Her face was slightly downcast, and though she was moving quick, like she always did, she wasn't moving quick enough, Samara thought, for her to feel danger was imminent.

"Miss Shepherd," she said, her voice weighted. "Good to see you again, my dear."

"It's good to see you, madam."

"Sit."

Samara waited for her to sit first.

"Miss Shepherd," said Clovinger, "I have good news, bad news, and another bit of news I hope you'll consider good. But I shall start with the bad."

"I'm ready, madam."

"My friend of over thirty years, the man you know as the Bird, died today in front of his office building in America. The official story from the Metrics government is that he had taken an energy shot which his heart could not handle. But the back of his watch was embedded with a small needle for just such an occasion, and just before he died, he had the presence of mind to activate it. He sent us a blood sample, which confirmed poisoning. His last act was very reflective of how he wanted to spend his life—gathering data in order to make the world a better place."

"I'm...very sorry to hear that." She was. For many reasons, not the least of which was that according to Denver and Jude, he was a very decent human being.

"Thank you. I'm sure he would have wanted to be around for the liberation, but I think he knew it was coming. I like to think he was comforted by that knowledge."

"Liberation?"

"That's the good news, Shepherd. I've been in meetings with our allies ever since I heard the recordings of that horrible man. We've made the executive decision to move forward with the invasion. Most of what I know is classified, but I can say that our strategy is largely hacker based. We'll shut down the technology that Metrics relies on to install a new government with as few casualties as possible. Hopefully none. I hope you won't be offended when I say this, Miss Shepherd, but our analysts say that it works to our advantage to have the people of America so very dependent on their government. They're used to being cared for, not used to having to stand up on their own. I don't think they'll fight us. And by this time next year, they'll have a government they simply count on to provide a safety net, not a birdcage. It'll be a cultural shock, but we have behavioral specialists working to ease the blow. That's my main priority, Shepherd, because I'm not at all worried about taking down the Ones. They're dependent on the technology, but they're not good at protecting themselves against a technological attack.

Samara wanted to burst into tears, or maybe jump up and down on the couch and muddy the yellow satin with her footprints, or dance wildly in and out through the drapes. Instead, she re-crossed her ankles. "Wonderful."

"That's the first bit of good news. The second is that your bill has been rushed through and is ready for a vote tonight. I've spoken with the Prime Minister, and he assures me that it has the votes to pass. You and your friends are safe here now. You'll be granted asylum when you apply, and you may stay as long as it takes to rebuild America. Personally, I hope you'll consider helping in the rebuilding efforts. I read your bill." Her eyes shone with something like pride as she leaned in. "The new United States will need a lot of new laws. I predict several will come from you."

Samara was speechless. She ran her tongue along the backs of her teeth, confirming that this was all real. "That's very good news. And...may I ask a question?"

"Please."

Samara took in a deep breath and held it there in her throat. "Is it possible to get information about my parents? If they survived?"

Clovinger seemed to allow gravity to soften her face downward. "I do not have an answer for you today, but I'll personally instruct our Director of Defense to look into it. I will notify you the minute I hear back."

She bit her tongue and choose a swirl on the carpet to focus her eyes on. "Thank you."

"One more thing." Clovinger stood and walked to the window with her hands clasped behind her back. "I treated you unfairly. I apologize." She turned around, and seemed to force herself to look at Samara. "I apologize."

CHAPTER THIRTY-SIX

BRISTOL HAD PLANNED TO DRESS IN HIS GRAY TWEED SUIT, BUT Cindy had something sent over at the last minute. This suit was a lighter material, brown, with a navy checkered shirt. He discarded the tie because he wanted to hold onto this feeling and manifest it physically: freedom.

She hadn't sent anything for Samara, and because Samara had refused to buy anything for herself, Bristol asked Denver and their mother to take her shopping and buy something for her when she wasn't looking. She could argue all she wanted, but she saved the whole damn world. The least he could do for her was buy her a dress.

At the reception, people ogled him, grabbed him, and pulled him into interesting conversations he would have felt stuck in before, but now felt at liberty to excuse himself when he noticed they were getting in too deep inside their own heads. Cindy and Albert were rock stars, explaining his work and encouraging opinionated conversation all night. Bristol kept looking at the french doors. The doors, paned in glass, were at the top of a short stairway and opened into a garden so Bristol could pretend he wanted to look at flowers if he needed to. He didn't want to. Finally, they all arrived together.

Denver, Mom, and Daniel first. Daniel wore an ill-fitting blue blazer, unbuttoned for comfort, and a pressed white shirt. Denver wore a black minidress and bright green heels, and Mom wore a calf-length black dress with neon pink shoes that matched Denver's. Behind them, Jude came in, wearing one of Bristol's old shirts—which actually fit him well. When do teenagers find the time to grow up? Finally, Samara walked through the door, dressed in floor-length silver tulle skirt and sleeveless navy top.

He met them halfway up the steps.

"How's everything going?" asked Denver.

"Very well. The champagne's nice and cold."

"Champagne?" asked Jude. "As if this wasn't already the best day of my life."

"Let's go to the bar." Denver locked arms with Daniel and Jude. "I think we've earned it."

They glided away, and Bristol took Samara's hand. "Let's go into the garden."

Samara laughed. "I just got here. And everyone's looking at us."

"That's why I want to leave."

She shrugged and smiled. "It's your night."

They walked out and stopped in front of a little rosebush encircled with white stones. He held her close to him and didn't let go.

"What?" she asked.

"Hmm?"

"I get the sense that you want to say something, but aren't saying it."

He blushed. "It's nothing I want to say. I was just thinking of something."

"Of what?"

"Just a little song that plays in my head every time you're close by. But I'm not much of a singer."

Samara smirked and leaned closer. "You have a few other gifts," she said, her lips softly brushing his.

He brought his cheek to hers.

"Life's storms may rudely blow,
Laying hope and pleasure low:
I'd ne'er deceive thee;
I can never, never leave thee."

THE END

Thank you for reading! Did you enjoy?

Please Add Your Review! And turn the page for a sneak peek of MUD, book 1 in the Chronicles of the Third Realm War!

SNEAK PEEK OF MUD

A STAIR CREAKS.

With the rain pounding down on the temple's rattling roof, the human may not have even heard the sound. But I do. It is too close, just outside the door of my tower. I look up from the Texts and listen.

There it is again.

A cold darkness tosses in my stomach.

Another stair creaks, and I know I'm about to kill again. The boiling thrill for blood rises within me and I know better than to bother suppressing it. It will happen anyway, no matter how much I try to bury the monster I really am.

Over the centuries, I've at least learned how to make it quick. My hand has already dug the box from the breast pocket of my cloak. I stride across my small room, my bare feet collecting dust. My back to the door, I lean on the mantle to lure the Hunter in. Then, I stare at the blank dusty wall and wait. The rustle of his cloak breaks the quiet with each step.

I want this over.

I hold the box high in my hand for him to see, as if I am

inspecting it. So small, so delicate. It nestles easily against my palm, comfortable and sure. It knows I must serve it.

Padded steps lift from the wood and onto the worn rug. My spine prickles with anticipation. Dread, heavy and thick like a storm cloud, wells up inside me. Have they learned nothing from their many losses? So many I cannot count them anymore.

I lay the box on the mantle for him to reach. My fingers itch for the fight, but I will not destroy the human of my own will. He must bring it on himself. I step away from it, leave it there for the Hunter to set his fate.

A rustle of rushed steps, a grunt, and a blade slices through my back, cool and slick. They keep trying to hurt me as if I were human, as if I felt the pain as they do. I reach around and remove the blade from my back. The skin knits itself back together.

I turn to him. Rain beats at the window. Wild dilated eyes peer up at me from under a deep red hood. Young. The cloak slips at his neck, too large for his growing body. It is the same deep red cloak all the others wore. Rich, dark, velvety, with the same gold braided trim. My own cloak, worn and ripped, seems even worse next to it.

The boy is trembling inside it. Waiting.

Has he even experienced a true fight before? Why did they send someone so young? Guilt twists through me.

"It's not too late. Leave." My voice is rough with disuse.

I shift the knife in my hand, holding it away to show him I don't mean him any harm, not if I can help it.

Like their cloaks, the Hunters' blades are fine, an elaborate pattern carved into its handle. It seems out of place in my hand, even after so many times. I run my fingers over its familiar ridges and wait. My ears are hot with anticipation, with dread of what I know comes next.

He gapes up at me, my monstrosity. I fight the urge to drop my gaze to the ground and instead keep my eyes locked on his. I try to will him to turn away, to go back to wherever he came from.

But I already know he won't. They never do.

Instead, he gives himself a quick shake and recovers his warrior's front. "The Sworn will not rest until it is destroyed. Give me the box."

Courage glows in his eyes. Strong. Fresh. What a waste of a life.

The Sworn? What is the Sworn?

"I cannot."

If only I could. It would save both of us.

He reaches for the box on the mantle.

"*Don't—*"

His fingers wrap around it.

The box's force takes over and my arms reach for him. I wince as my hand slips the Hunter's own blade through his soft middle. In the back of my mind, years and years of all the others who came before him flash through my memory. My hands buzz with mad hunger for the fight.

But it's already over.

He gasps, clasps his hands to his open belly, trying to hold it in. Then he slumps to the floor, spilling his life across the wooden panels. He opens his mouth to gasp, but it comes out as more of a gurgle, blood rising in his throat.

Not much time left. I try to push down the throbbing anger, the monster in me that hungers for the fight. I kneel beside him, gripping his head urgently so he is looking at me.

I hold the box to his face. "What is in it? Why do you come for it? Who are the Sworn?"

A red line dribbles down his chin. He looks up at me, trembling, shakes his head side to side.

"You don't know?"

His words come out in a hoarse whisper. He is shaking all over now in a struggle for his life. He opens his mouth again, tries to push out more. But the dark puddle grows fast below him, and it is over before it begins. Again, I am alone in the heavy dark of the temple tower.

****

The Hunter's eyes are cold and dead and open wide.

Watching, judging, condemning.

And they should. They have seen what I am.

I used to tell myself I would get used to it. I got used to snapping bones, last cries, pools of blood. But the eyes. The eyes freeze in an echo of their final panic and pain. When they realize these are their last breaths. Paled. Filmed. Hollow.

The Hunter's eyes stare up at me and I can't bear it.

I step out onto the balcony to escape them. Try to clear my head, still buzzing and grainy from the kill. Rain squeezes out of the sky like teardrops over the cobblestone streets in the marketplace below, over the thin rotted roofs of the laborers' quarters beyond it, over the wall that traps them within the city's borders. Even over the city center, where Epoh's elite rest, safe and dry. It pounds down on me, drop, by drop, by drop.

So close, yet again.

I set the box next to me on the railing, finger the curves of the delicate patterns painted over it. Such beauty. But it's what's inside that the Hunters come for, die for. That much I know. If only it would open. If only I knew what my body betrayed me for, why my hands are covered in blood yet again.

They will send another. They always do. I will be waiting. It goes without end, back further than I can remember. Centuries. Years trudge by, bodies pile up, the weight grows heavier.

I cling to my new clue. *The Sworn.* The phrase is meaningless to me, but it's a little more than I had before. Next time, maybe I can learn even more, if they keep sending their young and untested.

Already the dark sky is lightening toward a troubled gray. Another weary day is here in the city of Epoh.

Which means I'll be stuck with the Hunter's cold stare all day. There's no time to move the body now. Soon Epoh's Silencers will be out, the city's guards who keep the order with fear and clubs. Ever since they burned down the Holy District and all the Texts so many years ago, anything related to the Three Gods makes them jump. Any sign of movement from a temple like this would trigger a full search of the grounds. Then where would I go? There's nothing else left beyond Epoh's walls. Nowhere else to go.

It wasn't always like this. The realm was happy once. There were tons of other cities like Epoh, and they were thriving. But something shifted in the Second Realm War.

Some say the Three saw the destruction and anger and hate that spread throughout the realm of Terath in the Second Realm War and abandoned it. Others say the Three themselves were on the battlefield, and They came with Their soldiers to beat at Epoh's wall, begging to be let in and shown a little of kindness—care for wounds, a drink of water—but the people would not let them in for fear of the rebels, and They gave up on us. Others say the Gods simply saw how few men dared fight for Them and turned away.

Whatever it was, the Gods are gone, and the people won't dare invoke Them for anything, afraid of Their wrath. The realm is in ruins. Only the Gods know what lies beyond Epoh's high walls. If They care enough to look.

That's why I hide here, in the temple. I keep to where the humans don't dare wander. The Gods don't worry me. They forgot this realm long ago.

I force myself back inside and quickly step toward the body. I drag my fingers over the grayed lids, closing them. I untie his cloak and pull it from under him to mop up the congealing blood from the floor. With his eyes off of me, my entire body finally begins to relax again.

It must be such great relief, knowing you can end. I envy them that, the humans. But not like this. Not before your time. Not alone, with no chance.

When I'm done with the floor, I lay the cloak over the body. His legs jut out at the end, the hand still pushing against the sliced organs. A grotesque empty shell.

The eyes still haunt me through the cloth. But there's no time to do anything more.

I pick up the Texts from the mantle and move quickly past the body to the window, trying to push the Hunter out of my thoughts. Below my feet the ornate rug, once rich and brilliant, is worn so deep I can feel the wood's grain under my toes. Decades of standing in the same place day after day after day. Here, I am in the shadows. A human peering in from the streets would not see me. But I can see out.

I watch them. Completely alone, silent, still, there is nothing else to do.

My temple tower rears up against what's left of the holy district, tall and tired, leering over the market. I watch each day play out on its wide streets and small carts. Behind it, the expired grandeur of the aged towers rises, a rotted reminder of a lost past.

There was a time when Epoh was Terath's shining jewel. Its streets bustled with life at all hours. But the Second Realm War changed everything. The First Creatures tore through the realm like it was paper, their battles destroying men's cities, homes, the land itself. And the men, they took part. Some stood up and fought for their Gods. But others turned away from them in anger. Others' loyalty was easily bought with magic, jewels, or promises of safety after it all ended. Still others ran, cowered, and just waited for it to end.

I'd never, in all my years, seen such destruction.

This is when Zevach arrived at Epoh, with his flock trailing behind him, desperate to believe his promises of protection and hope. Then Zevach told his followers if they wanted the city, they must take it for themselves. Desperate and scared, they fought their way in and destroyed most of its people.

They should have known then what he would become, that this is the city's fate. I should have.

The sky turns from pitch black to a troubled gray. The rays of light touch over the battered city. Silencers' boots tap against the pavement. Another weary day in Epoh is here.

Don't stop now. Keep reading with your copy of MUD available now.

Want even more dystopian adventures? Try Chronicles of the Third Realm War by City Owl Author, E. J. Wenstrom!

Torn apart by war and abandoned by the gods, only one hope remains to save humanity. But the savior isn't human at all.

Trapped by his Maker's command to protect a mysterious box, Adem is forced to kill anyone who tries to steal it. When a young boy chances upon Adem's temple, he resists temptation, intriguing the golem. As the boy and his sister convince Adem to leave the refuge of his temple, the group lands in a web of trouble. Now Adem will do whatever necessary to keep his new young charges safe, even if it means risking all to get rid of the box. Their saving grace comes in the form of an angel who offers to set Adem free of the box's magic by granting his greatest desire—making him human. But first, Adem must bring back the angel's long-dead human love from the Underworld. In doing so, he will risk breaking the barrier between the realms, a cataclysm that could launch the Third Realm War. To set things right, he may be forced to give up the only thing he's ever truly wanted...a chance at a soul of his own.

Thank you for reading! For more from Megan Lynch, check out her website and join the mailing list.

Facebook: www.facebook.com/mlriggs

Twitter: www.twitter.com/mlynchbooks

Instagram: www.instagram.com/m.lynch.books/

Website: www.mlynch.net

Please sign up for the City Owl Press <u>newsletter</u> for chances to win special subscriber-only contests and giveaways as well as receiving information on upcoming releases and special excerpts.

All reviews are **welcome** and **appreciated**. Please consider leaving one on your favorite social media and book buying sites.

For books in the world of romance and speculative fiction that embody Innovation, Creativity, and Affordability, check out City Owl Press at <u>www.cityowlpress.com</u>.

ACKNOWLEDGMENTS

It takes a village to raise a book, and I'll forever be grateful for the little village that worked so hard to bring this one into the hands of readers. Working on the story of Bristol, Samara, Denver, and Jude has kept my heart humming over these past few years, and I'm overjoyed to express my gratitude to the following people for their invaluable support:

To Jen Chesak, who, from the day she read the abysmal version of the first chapter of the first book, saw potential in it and encouraged me to dedicate the time it would take to revise. Thank you for sticking with me throughout this entire series with patience and heartfelt critique.

To Amanda Roberts, who plucked this story from her slush pile and shepherded me into the world of publishing, I'll be forever grateful for your expertise and guidance.

To the entire team at City Owl Press, especially Tina Moss, Yelena Casale, and Marianne Hull. You guys are an author's dream. Driven but kind, motivational but grounded, you are all just really unique people, and it's no surprise that that uniqueness shines through in your company.

To my local critique group, WorD: meeting with you in Rickert and Beagle is my regular reminder that I'm not the only crazy one to imagine worlds and hang out with imaginary friends. Thanks for that! Special thanks to Jamie Lackey, Aaron Roth, JD Barker, Kevin Hayes, and Karen Yun-Lutz.

To my family: Dad, Brian, Kevin, Jamie, Nanny, Rich, Lindsay, Tim, Ellie, and Michael, and a huge shoutout to Mom and Dianne, who babysat so I could write.

Finally, to my husband, Ryan, and our children, Finnegan and Clark. Ryan, thank you for removing my fear of being fully devoted to your heart's purposes, because every day you demonstrate your full devotion to mine.

ABOUT THE AUTHOR

MEGAN LYNCH lives in Nashville, Tennessee with her husband and her sons, Finnegan and Clark. Her debut dystopian novel, Unregistered, depicts the underside of a utopian society when some members live on the fringe and don't fit in. In addition to writing, she loves reading, running, yoga, music, and human rights.

www.mlynch.net

ABOUT THE PUBLISHER

City Owl Press is a cutting edge indie publishing company, bringing the world of romance and speculative fiction to discerning readers.

www.cityowlpress.com